Falling from the Strings

It's *odd* how reality can be so disappointing,
even though it's dreams that make life worth living.

a novel by
H.J. Duffey

Falling from the Strings

ISBN: 978-0-578-66944-1

Printed in the United States of America

Special thanks to Adam Layton, Courtney Waldron, and Becca Newman

Contents

Introduction

AT THE FRONT TABLE IN THE BAR I sat alone, staring at my drink, watching as the ice slowly melted. Cool water droplets slowly slid down the glass and onto the table. The server didn't give me a coaster, so the drink had its chance to stain the table, and when I laid my hand on it I found it was sticky. Disgusting. How can someone think this is okay? I pulled my hand away, and the table kept the dead skin, leaving behind a blotched mirror image of the side of my hand.

Looking around the room, I saw pairs of people laughing, smiling together as they chatted. Making new memories with one another, solidifying bonds. It's not fair; why do they get to feel joy? Why do they get to be happy? I long for that feeling. I could be in a crowd and still be all on my lonesome. Looking back at the handprint, seeing a copy of me on a surface, it hurt. Because even though I'm alone, I will always have a stabbing pain whispering in my ear. It tells me how we are better than these little things, these animals. I try to ignore it, but the voice bangs around in my head. It's hard to focus. Its thoughts mix with mine. Sometimes it's hard to tell who's in control. It's a constant battle.

Taking a sip of my drink, I look at the bartender, and It had to comment.

"Ugh, how can something as ugly as that be able to stand there and act like it belongs," It mocked.

"Please ... just ... shut up." I rubbed my eyes.

1

"I mean look at him. All that blubber. What is he even doing?" It grunted.

"His job."

"His job? Pouring whiskey into a glass is not a job. A child could pour whiskey into a glass."

"For fucks' sake, let me drink in peace!" I shouted.

The room went silent. A waitress asked if I was okay.

"Um, yeah. Sorry about the noise. I-I was just talking to myself. Won't happen again."

"Okay ... ?" The waitress walked away.

I was still getting a few confused looks from others. Whatever. They'll just chalk it up to some freak losing his mind.

"Nice job. Nothing weird about talking to a voice in your head," It said sarcastically.

I finished my drink and left a twenty on the table, escaping out into the cold blue night.

1: Uniquely Average Day

EVERY MORNING THAT ANNOYING ALARM made that screeching call, and every morning was worse than the one before.

The exhaust-fumed air was quite pleasant to take in. The screaming alarm clock, not so much. It took about 5 minutes to get out of bed, and that's when the migraine started to settle in.

First up, the basic necessities:

The shower was freezing cold. With my big toe, I turned the shower faucet clockwise. A few seconds later it was steaming. The scalding water running down my face felt disconcertingly delightful, feeling my skin burn. Wouldn't it be nice if the water just boiled me alive? Then I wouldn't have to deal with the throbbing pain called life. By the time I finished showering, the bathroom might as well have been a sauna.

The process of cleaning my teeth was never a pleasant operation. Flossing was never an enjoyable experience, more like a thousand tiny knives. Every few seconds, I had to let out a silent scream. Brushing my teeth was never fun, scrubbing across my fangs, blood would mix in with the foamy paste, like a rabid dog. To finish off, a simple mouthwash tasted like shit, but the pain was weirdly soothing – better than being a toothless worm I suppose.

Every morning face cream would be applied to the forehead, cheeks, nose, and chin. The bags under the eyes needed several layers to keep them at bay. As far as I can tell, the advertising was a lie. The

3

reflection was disgusting. I looked like a bat with its eyeballs turned inside out. Splashing water on my face didn't help; if anything it made it worse. Even after the wretched teeth cleaning, morning breath was still apparent. I smeared the deodorant on and moved onto more important items.

By that time, I could somewhat understand my surroundings. Walking into the living room, I tripped over an empty scotch bottle. There was a sense of despair in the air whispering to me, *Maybe today is the day.* Doubtful. Try not to get too excited.

"It would be much easier to stay home and avoid everyone," It said.

Next on the list was to get dressed into some fair clothing. This was one of the few highlights of the day. A shoe is not just a shoe. A shirt is not just a shirt. Humans are in a constant state of choice and judgement. When presenting oneself, there is a snap judgement by the people around you. Clothing is one of the few things that shows me for who I really am. Look at children in elementary school – there is a segregation between who is rich and who is filth. The little brats who wear expensive clothing, those are the ones whose parents use them as tiny trophies, as a way of saying, "I am better than you." The kids who wear old raggedy hand-me-downs, those are the kids with parents who can't waste money on the hot new fashion statement. The difference between a poor child who grows up and becomes substantial versus a rich kid staying rich is in the way they carry themselves. An Oxford-born man sees his apparel as nothing more than the clothes on his back, but a slum-born kid learns to hold his stance. A slum boy knows the reality, and he knows how quickly it can be taken away. To make one mistake in the way he presents himself is worse than eternal damnation.

Scrolling through the hanging clothes in the walk-in closet, I found a coal-black blazer with a matching pair of pants. Flipping through my vast collection of shirts, I found a silver-gray button-up. The tie that followed had a coal-like shading, but was a bit on the cool side. I checked for any loose threads or tears. Putting it on, I began to feel omnipotent. The suit hugged me, not too tight, just enough to show off a bit of definition. Grabbing the shoe polish from a shelf, I scrubbed the leather boots, blacking every corner and crevice, not leaving even a microscopic trace of weakness. Re-knotting the tie, it took me five attempts before it was acceptably knotted. Examining my image in the mirror, the only thing reflecting back was greatness. Sadly, though, reality settled in a few seconds later, and it was time for breakfast.

Walking into the kitchen, I put on my full-body plastic suit. Turning the stove top on, I lathered a pan in olive oil. While waiting for the pan to heat up, I opened the fridge; I retrieved an onion, green peppers, crumbled roquefort, and two eggs. The side door held some wine – not the good stuff, but I'd found it on discount. Dicing the onions and green peppers, I nicked my finger. Blood dripped onto the cutting board in an abstract pattern. Using my index finger, I dipped it in the blood splatter and drew a smiley face. I don't understand how people can do that. It hurts to even try it.

After cleaning the cut and putting a bandage on it, I mixed the vegetables with the egg and the roquefort. When pouring it into the pan, there was a slight sizzle. As I waited for the omelet to cook, I noticed a glass sitting on the counter top. It was too much work to pour a glass of wine. Drinking straight from the bottle would be much easier, cutting costs, saving the environment. The omelet was done. Sliding it onto a plate, I took a seat at the table. Last week's paper had one interesting headline, "Crisis in America." When is there not?

Finally, done with the morning routine, I walked out and got in the car. It reeked of dead rat. Still drowsy, I acknowledged that it was time to tackle the godawful "festival" called work. Passing by the far-too-familiar buildings, I noticed a homeless man at an upcoming intersection. He wore a winter coat, a dirty pink cap with gaping holes that let what little hair he had peek out. His face was horrific. Several teeth were missing and there was a gruesome mole the size of a child's thumb buried beneath the hair of his left eyebrow. To finish his ensemble was a gray beard with a dark pink line running down the center chin hairs.

The driver in the car in front of me rolled down a window and handed the bum some money. I, on the other hand, did my best to avoid making eye contact with him.

Don't look at me. Don't look at me. Don't look at me, staring down at the steering wheel.

"Don't give him money, you don't know what he's going to do with it. He might just spend it on something useless, like a glow stick," It grunted.

Eventually the light turned green, and I tried not to speed off like a maniac.

I parked the car a block away from work, and thought there might as well have been a sign screaming this day was going to be painful. Taking one step into the office, first obstacle was Phil, my so-called "friend," greeting me with his annoying smile.

"Hey Lib, what's up man, anything interesting happen over the weekend?" Phil said this with an enormous level of enthusiasm in his voice, along with what looked to be blueberry muffin in his teeth.

Phil was the type of guy who came to work barely meeting the dress code, which was a buttoned up shirt with a pair of jeans. Phil preferred to wear skinny jeans though, hoping his package would look twice its size. I was certain he stuffed his pants with socks. Not only did he look like a total douche, but he also talked as if he were a stud. Even a total idiot could tell that he was merely a wannabe ladies man, a womanizer in his own mind. It's fair to assume in his downtime he watched gangster shows and scoured the internet for *tips on how to pick up chicks*. His favorite thing to do at work was to tell me stories about his sexual encounters with some depressed women from the night before. I don't truly know if the women were actually depressed. I just assumed, because they hooked up with Phil, and Phil is repulsive.

Some of his stories seemed to have too much detail to be true. It's as if Phil was a salesman, working his ass off to show you how great his product is. In this case, Phil's product is in his pants, and he was trying to sell it to any woman he could see, smell, or hear.

I tried to pump out a little pep and said, "Um, nothing much, just the usual," but it just came out as irritated boredom. Or bored irritation.

"Bro, you totally missed out! So I went to this old run-down bar, and this girl is totally eyeing me, dude. So I go up to her, and compliment her on that fine ass she was carrying. But then she throws her drink in my face."

"Hmmm, seems like a waste of alcohol to me," I said.

"Wait! I'm not done, bro! So, I do the whole fake apology routine, and she buys it. So I buy her a drink, and the next thing you know, we're breaking in my new bed!" Phil said, raising his hand, waiting for a high five. I didn't give him the satisfaction.

After that eternity of a conversation, I shuffled toward my desk, stopping by the water machine for a quick drink. Once again, some imbecile tried to talk to me.

"Lib, I need you to get me the Johnson account as soon as possible, okay great! Thanks!" my boss Linda exclaimed.

Linda is the basic stereotypical dense TV white girl. Always talking in long drones, always holding a drink in her hand, and always looking at her reflection. One time a colleague of mine asked for two minutes of her time, but she told him she was busy. I was behind her looking over her shoulder; she was doodling cats on her clipboard.

"Huh," I told her, "yeah, okay."

"You feeling all right?" she asked, putting her hand on my shoulder.

"Why don't you fuck off and mind your own business?" It said, butting into my conversation.

"Yeah, just getting hyped for the day," she said, huffing a bit as she shrugged her hand off me.

At my desk, falling back in the swivel chair, plugging in my music, life felt insufferable, but slightly better than yesterday. The desktops were becoming outdated, and the screens had mold growing inside of them. Not wanting to work yet, I tried to beat my *The Tower of Hanoi* record; it stood at four minutes eleven seconds.

"Damn it."

By this time the computer has become fully capable for use, but that didn't matter. Not beating my record left a sour taste in my mouth.

As I was scrolling through spam and work emails, something strange arrived in my inbox – a message from an old high school acquaintance, asking to catch up. It was immediately deleted, and then to take more precautions, I deleted it again from the trash box.

It wasn't until an hour later that I actually got any work done.

I made a brief scan over the Johnson account, and everything seemed to add up, all but for a little convenience store west of downtown called Sullivan's Station. Their cleaning expenses were through the roof.

My first thought was *Should I tell Linda?*

"But how can they spend three thousand dollars on cleaning supplies?" I whispered to myself.

"And how does this affect you?" It said, voicing its own opinion.

"I never asked for your opinion."

Looking up, I could see Linda was in her office playing with her hair.

"Wouldn't it be nice to just pop those little eyes out and just stomp on them, turn them into jelly?

The office would praise you for it!" It told me, trying to be enthusiastic.

Walking over to Linda's personal office, with the Johnson account folders, someone decided to tap me on the shoulder. My body couldn't help but shudder. It was Phil again.

"Hey Phil."

"Phil is the most boring name in existence. I'd rather swim the Atlantic Ocean then have to be around someone named Phil. Do you know how many people out there probably hate their parents for naming them Phil? I imagine 99.99 percent of them resent them for it, with the other .01 percent having already changed their names to something like James or Michael – and they then moved to Canada to hide their dreadful past."

Reality kicked me in the face, though, when Phil started talking about something else that I didn't care about.

"Are you even listening to me?" Phil suddenly asked, a concerned look on his face.

"Sorry, what did you say?" I still was not giving him my full attention.

"Ugh, the presentation that we're giving. You know, the one that could push us up that corporate ladder? Do you have the flash drive?"

"Oh yeah ... let me grab it." I shuffled back to my desk.

I put the Johnson account back in a desk drawer for safekeeping.

"Remember, a smile can get you far in this world," Phil said, showing me his pearly whites, with the blueberry still front and center.

Smiling was not my strong suit. It probably looked like something right out of *Clockwork Orange,* and Phil's reaction was not agreeable.

"You know what, don't smile then, just look like you're trying to be professional, okay? But not so much that you are mocking them. Also, wipe that douchey look off your face."

"But this is my normal face." Slightly offended, I didn't bother trying to argue with him.

Suddenly, the outer door swung open, and two men and a woman, all dressed in black suits, walked in like royalty. They took a seat in the three chairs parallel to me and Phil. Phil wiped his hands on his pants, and went to shake their hands. I just stood there, waiting for this hell to be over. Phil walked back to where he had been standing and started babbling on, leaving me to zone out and stare at the floor. It wasn't until about five minutes later that my eyes rolled up from looking at the floor, seeing everyone staring at me. The PowerPoint on the screen said "Estimated Stock Value for Next Quarter" along with a graph with a rigid line with an arrow at the end pointing upward.

"As you can plainly see, our company has been increasing its value of stock from the past year, and by looking at the materials that are going to be released next quarter we were able to calculate what the consumer market will want from us, and we converted the amount of profits into stock holdings value." Phil exclaimed over this with pride in his voice.

"Interesting," one of the men said.

"Yeah, it would be if it were true," I whispered to myself.

11

"Excuse me?" the woman said.

"Oh, it's nothing ... Well, the idea that you can calculate the value of the company's stock based on its sales revenue sounds nice, but where are liabilities and the capital? You're just looking at this from a goods being sold point of view, instead you should look at the company in a way that it's dependent on everyone else, which in a way we are. At no point did he mention the p/e ratios, or the annual dividends per share. What about the company's public appearance? If he would've factored in even one of those it would indicate a far different graph than this thing he pulled out of the trash."

The room fell silent. A few seconds later, the woman asked, "So what you are trying to say is that next quarter our company is going to lose more than just profits?"

"Um no," I told her, "I'm trying to say that we should look at the big picture pieces, not just some products that are going to be released."

The woman made a "hmmm" noise as she typed away on her phone. Without another word, she walked out. The two men followed behind.

The door made a loud bang as it closed. A little confused by what had just happened, I started to pack up my stuff.

"What was that all about?" Phil demanded.

"Maybe they went to go get lunch. Do we just wait for them to come back?"

"No, what? What was that whole thing about dividends and that other shit? You made me look like an idiot!" Phil pouted.

"What? That? It's the basis of the market world," I said on my way out.

"Where are you going?" Phil demanded, shouting at me from down the hall.

"Lunch."

Is there ever a situation where you always both love and hate an activity? That's my life every day from 11 to 1 o'clock, waiting in lines and bumping into all of these morons. These ordinary people on the sidewalk live such illogical lives.

"Oh my gosh! Did you hear that Jason may be cheating on Britney?"

or

"Excuse me, but you gave me an extra caramel on my coffee instead of whip cream."

It's frustrating to be the only sane person: watching people waste their valuable time on new trends, and what's new in fashion – the stench is gag worthy. Every once in a while, a tear will run down my face because of it.

Finding a place to eat wasn't easy. Originally, lunch was the best, because it was at my desk, but apparently, I eat too loudly, and it annoys everyone else. So an ultimatum was offered – either eat lunch with Linda, or go somewhere else. I chose the lesser of the two evils, and decided to surround myself with people I don't hate yet. Truly, eating lunch alone is far better than eating with coworkers.

Steak? Sushi? Tacos? There are too many choices to pick from. After a block or two, walking past a window, I noted a very interesting picture of a noodle with a smiley face on it. The drawing itself was horrendous, but the idea was interesting enough to catch my attention. As I shoved open the door, an unfamiliar scent caught me off guard. The only way that it could be described was if the smell of old books and hot dog water made a baby. Oddly enough, it wasn't really a bad smell. If anything, it lured me in.

The line moved along quickly. Skimming over the menu on the wall, I saw the most compelling choice was soup called "tien khan." I ordered a bowl and paid for it, and the cashier handed me a small metal rod with a piece of paper taped on it that said number 11.

I took a seat at a table in the corner, waiting for my soup to come. The people noise around me was bothersome. Picking a random song to focus on instead, I found the music was toe-tap worthy. Looking around at all the décor, it was obvious that it had an Asian theme. Whether it was Chinese, Japanese, or some other culture was beyond me. There were dragons painted on the wall that spanned the whole restaurant. The dragons were intricately detailed – there were probably thousands or hundreds of thousands of scales painted on one dragon. Their eyes felt like a reminder of death, yet at the same time of hope. The biggest dragon's face resembled a shar-pei dog. A few minutes went by and boredom settled in.

A man stood in line, looking outlandish and jumpy. His hands were in his coat pockets. Someone screamed.

"All right listen up! This is robbery! No one try to be a hero, or someone is going to get shot!"

"You have got to be kidding me ..." It complained.

Raising my hand like an elementary school boy, I said to the robber, "Excuse me sir, but can you just come back in like thirty minutes? I'd rather not have to deal with a dumbass like you today."

"Excuse me?" He stomped over to me, puffing out his chest.

"Actually yes, you see I don't have the time ..."

"No, no, no, no, see that's not how this works! Now listen closely, you are going to grab your wallet out of your pocket, and give me all the money you have." He was flinging his gun around, pointing it at my face.

"The thing is ..." I started once again and the robber cut me off, this time by pulling the hammer back on his revolver, not three feet from my face.

Doing as he said, I stood up and pulled my wallet out, took out the money, and held it out to him. As he reached for it, I kicked him where it hurts, causing him to fall to the ground, misfiring his gun. Unluckily for me, the bullet barely missed my shoulder. He tried to stagger to his feet, but I kicked him back down. He dropped the gun, and I used the metal menu rod to stab his head. Blood spurted onto the floor, and the other customers gasped and swore. One woman wailed loudly. I grabbed the revolver from the guy, unloading all the bullets except one. I hated the sound of the spinning cylinder, bringing back memories of what could have been.

Isn't it great how you're just having a terrible day, and then things start to look up? Pity he missed. Funny how people will change their attitudes when they've got a gun pointed at their head.

"Wait! Wait! Wait! I was just kidding, man!" the robber said, waving his hands in the air.

"Oh really. In that case," I pulled the trigger, making a click.

"Oh God! Please, I'll give you whatever you want!" he pleaded.

"Fantastic." I aimed at his head and pulled the trigger, still with only a loud click.

By this time, the fully-grown man was sobbing in front of me, hugging my ankles, begging me to spare his life. Once again, I pulled the trigger, and still his brains weren't splattered on the floor.

"I'll give you anything you want! Please stop!" he screamed.

"You know what I want? You know what I want? I want you to get the hell out of this place, and leave me alone. Next time don't fucking miss!"

I waved him toward the front doors.

He scrambled up and ran out the door and out of sight. The other customers started cheering.

"Shut up!" I wailed.

The café quickly became silent.

I walked over to pick up my soup, and I tipped the cashier with a little bent rod and a revolver.

I sat back down and someone tapped me on the shoulder. A little boy handed me a napkin, and pointed at his ear. There was a loud ringing, and what felt to be something wet on my ear. Wiping the napkin on it, I discovered blood was draining like a fountain, most likely from the gunfire, causing a rupture in the eardrum. I held the napkin there, finished my soup, and twirled up the napkin to make a sort of cork for my ear. As I walked back to work, the music in my head was the only thing to distract me from the temptation of jumping into speeding traffic.

My phone buzzed. Looking at the screen, the name said "Mom" and I let it go to voicemail I walked on.

When I reached the office, Linda stopped me and asked why she hadn't gotten the Johnson account yet. She then started lecturing me on how she understands that it's hard to keep up with the pace around here. The reality was, I could have had that report and five others done before noon. I just chose not to.

"Why is there a napkin in your ear?" Linda said looking confused, as usual.

"Wouldn't it be nice to see her head on a stake?" It whispered in my ear.

"Oh, a guy was pointing a gun at me," I told her. The misfire ..."

Linda looked surprised and then giggled a little.

"Oh my gosh, that is hilarious, your jokes are so funny! You almost got me there! Almost like last time, making me think that Transylvania was a real place, but I've learned from your tricks! Not this time." She was laughing way too hard.

I walked over to my desk, and I handed her the Johnson account. We then made uncomfortable eye contact, as if she were trying to look into my soul. Creepy.

Zoning out, I found that music was a good distraction. There was still at least two hours left until I could go home. Because I tolerated this job, I decided to get some actual work done. Whizzing through the computer, opening documents, reading them, and sending out status reports to the higher-ups, it did make time go by faster. There was still too much time left in the day though. What else was there to do? Take a nap. As my eyes rolled down and my mind eased blankly into a discomfort bliss, another irritant decided to whisper in my ear.

"Wake up, boner boy."

Bennett, my other boss, had his crotch in front of my face.

He was the worst thorn in my ass. If he dropped off the face of the earth, life would be only slightly better. He spends his free time eating the gunk under his fingernails, and harasses anyone he considers a threat to his masculinity. He is the actual reason that there is a hole in the wall back at my house. One time, I saw him actually take money out of a beggar's hat. I may not give the guy money, but to actually take it from a bum is far worse.

"Where's the Johnson account? It needs a little look-over with these eyes." he said, cleaning out his ear with his pinky.

"Well, if you mean the Johnson account, I don't have it, Linda does."

"Is that sass I'm detecting? You know, I could replace you just as fast as I can snap my fingers."

"Well, as I said, Linda has it."

"Linda! Shit, she is one hot piece of ass," he said with a little drool running down his lip.

"Okay," and I swiveled my chair away to avoid the tent he was pitching.

"What, you don't like the human anatomy? Psh, most of you people probably don't even know what your who-ja-wonkies are actually even for." He said this while making seriously inappropriate gestures.

There were some scissors in my middle left drawer. *Just think of the possibilities.* "I can think of ten different uses for those scissors, not one being cutting paper." I could feel its anger.

I decided to leave and hide in a bathroom stall, knowing from experience that Bennett would only continue to grind the air next to me if I sat still. Only thirty minutes left until the work day was over. Because there is nothing to do in the bathroom, other than what it's meant for, I decided my best option was to just sit in my stall with the door locked, wait it out for a half hour and listen to music.

But it seems like whenever life is going well, something bad has to happen. My favorite song came on, and right on cue a woman barges in to the men's room, bawling her eyes out. For about a minute, I tried to ignore it, but it just got louder and louder. What else was there to do, except walk out of the stall and ask her to please grieve in silence, which is exactly what I did.

Her initial reaction was stunned, discovering she was indeed in the men's room. She then went back to crying.

"Okay, what happened?" I was only asking in hopes I could get rid of her.

"I just turned thirty-one today, and no one said anything! I mean, I'm basically now an old sack of garbage! My boobs are starting to fall down and I think I'm starting to go bald!" she said, choking on her words, still making that ugly contracting face.

"Okay first of all, getting older means that you are living longer. I'm not a mind reader, but I assume you want to live longer, right? Secondly, you do look a bit puffy. So, maybe eat a salad. Third of all, and the most important, if you are going to resume crying, can you please at least do it in the women's restroom?"

"What the hell? You are really saying that to me right now?" She started wiping her tears away, replacing them with a face rapidly shifting to rage.

"So, we are good here. Okay bye." I walked back into the stall, closed the door, and locked it.

The distraught woman slammed the door on her way out.

The drive home was quiet. Getting in, the first thing to do was to sit on the couch and relax. After a while I got up and made myself a steak, along with lightly drizzled caesar salad. In the middle of my meal my phone started to ring. The caller ID said "Mom" again. Clicking the answer button, I say in my signature boring tone, "Hey." Immediately, she started rambling on about how she wants to come visit. I quickly changed the subject, and asked about how her retirement was going. Instantly, she started talking about basket weaving. It became too much of a struggle to follow, so I zoned out, and said "oh" and "ya" and "mhmm" every once in a while. About ten minutes later, I came back to reality from a simple question. "So, what did you do today?"

"Oh, just the usual, dealing with the drunken typicals at the counter."

"Please, just be careful. I don't want my baby to get hurt," she said, in her concerned baby talk voice.

"All right, I gotta go. My manager is hounding me on taking phone calls." I clicked off and tossed the phone to the side of me.

Fucking die already, I whispered.

The clock says 8:27 p.m. Shuffling into my room, I change into some sports shorts and head out for a jog. It's now dark out. Sweat rolls down my cheek, and my breathing becomes more aggressive. I spot a few broken bottles on the sidewalk. Some cigarette butts sit next to the trash cans, waiting to be picked up by a good Samaritan. A few rats scurry in the alley, squeaking while I jog by. There is a basketball court ahead, and a group of teenagers are playing. Standing on the sidelines, I watch as the giants play their little game.

My vision started to go blurry, and a flash of darkness overwhelmed me. Suddenly, I was standing in the middle of the cold dark woods. A brawny shadow figure stood a few yards ahead of me. After a few seconds of processing – or trying to process – what had just happened, I took a closer look at the figure, not sure what it was, and discovered it was a man with his back to me.

"Hey." I hesitate to speak.

No response.

"Hey!" louder now.

The shadowy man didn't move a muscle.

"Hey, asshole," I said, becoming pissed.

21

My patience ran out, and I stomped over to him, forcing him to turn around. When I grabbed his shoulder, though, my hand sank through him like smoke, and he disappeared in the wind. I leaped back, rubbing my eyes, thinking they'd deceived me, but the man was actually gone.

A loud screeching erupted from the sky, metallic, sounding like a runaway train trying to come to a never-ending stop. The noise was unbearable. I couldn't hear myself think. My head felt like it was going to explode. My vision went blurry.

Lying on the cold concrete, befuddled by what had happened, I watched as someone walked over to me. He asked if I was okay.

I told him to fuck off.

"Whatever, man." And he went back to his game.

The time was 10:25 p.m., nearly 11 o'clock by the time I got home, suffocating myself in the sheets.

To put this in perspective, I probably have some permanent hearing loss in my left ear, and I made a new enemy at work, and all in all, this day was absolute shit.

2: Dreamland

TOSSING AND TURNING IN BED, I find that sleep is not an option. Something always seems to be wrong. Either a heatwave or frostbite. My mouth is dry. My lips are chapped. Did I forget to lock all the doors? Is the alarm set? All of these thoughts were driving me insane.

Not to sound optimistic, but the only option left was to shut my eyes and hope for the best.

Deep breaths in and out. In and out. In and out. Slowly relaxing my body, letting the covers suffocate me.

Opening my eyes, I found myself floating in an abyss, soaking in an unfathomable desperation, hoping my dreams come true. Nothing new. I shut my eyes again, knowing this was where I belonged.

There was a small thud. Why not change the scenery, take me to a place where no one belongs? The room had no windows, no doors, no furniture, just a white covering. One side had a bright glow to it, the other was dark and provoking.

"How's the ear?" a deep grunting voice asked.

"Fine," I respond, looking at the dark side of the room, making out a fatal outline of my friend crouched in the corner.

"Don't lie. We both know it hurts like hell."

"Then why even ask? My day was great by the way, thanks for asking."

"Don't try to act all high and mighty. You know, your eardrum wouldn't even be shattered if you would've just shot the guy," It said in a quiet monotone.

"No, actually it wouldn't." I tried not to let him get a rise out of me.

"Doesn't matter, if I was out there, then we would be living our dream. No more working at that boring job. No more dealing with pricks like Bennett. No more problems."

"Yeah well, I wouldn't be here if it weren't for you, so thanks," I said sarcastically. "Just be grateful I let you listen in on my conversations. Besides, you don't have anywhere to be anytime soon."

Silence.

"Did you know cannibalism is quite common throughout the animal kingdom? Humans think it's disgusting only because of social conduct. I just think it's funny. Imagine a rabbit, one of those little white furballs, nibbling on one of its own brothers or a sister."

"What's your point?"

"My point is that PEOPLE always expect to be saved, but to survive you need to take matters into your own hands.

All this chatter amongst one another, pretending to care, ugh, it's nauseating."

"Most people would call that normal."

"Is it now? Well tell me, if I wasn't part of you, would those PEOPLE still be alive? Would that restaurant owner still have his money? Would there be one less threat out there? I gave us purpose. You play with these animals as if there's nothing wrong. We both know that can only last so long."

I paced back and forth.

"No! You're just a problem, a parasite, trying to infect me from the inside out. If you had some kind of control, then you would have pulled the trigger. I'm in control! Not you, me!"

"Sometimes I wonder how much you must hate me, but then I remember, I'm all you have. So don't pretend to be this gospel all-knowing person. You're just as bad."

"Shut up!"

"Do everyone a favor, and stop lying to yourself. It doesn't suit you. Sure, I may be seen as an extremist, but that's what the world is now."

"Don't test me or ..."

"Or what? I'm tired of listening to you blabber on. Just loosen up a bit. God! You do the same shit every day, and the one time something tweaks your perfect schedule, the whole world collapses! Why not just enjoy the ride? Do me a favor, when you wake up, take that stick out of your ass, and do something new for once."

Turning away, staring at the wall, "How about you stay locked in here, and I'll be trapped out there. How's that for compromise?"

The shadow jumps at me, but before his fingers can wrap around my throat, the darkness pulled him back to the cold dark corner.

"Coward! Look at me when I'm talking to you! Look at me!" He cried, trying to claw at me. "This is just as much my world in here as it is yours! You hate those animals you call people! They're all just insects that need to be shown the right path!"

"This right here ... this is why you'll never leave this place. You aren't ready for the outside world, and never will be. Now if you excuse me, I think I shall give myself a break. From you," I said.

With a snap of a finger, a door shape hole revealed itself in the wall.

"Lib! Wait! Don't go! Don't leave me." His voice gushed with misery. A sparkling tear slid down his disgusting face, smudging onto the floor.

"I'll see you tomorrow." I walked out of the room.

"Lib ... just take my advice. Just this once," he pleaded.

For a brief moment I could see how sad and desperate he truly was.

26

"I'll think about it." And with a snap of my finger, the hole sealed itself shut.

This new room had nothing special to it, no difference in shade or color. A white canvas. It needed something to make it pop. I started punching the wall as hard as I could. My fist became a paintbrush, making a masterpiece of red. Knuckles crunched as bone broke through the skin. The pain was quite displeasing, but after putting on the final touches, a beautiful array of red covered the walls. With one hand mangled, bone sticking out like claws, blood dripping onto the floor. Healing it would be easy, just a thought away, but the pain was the only true feeling I had left. So with one hand to spare, I snapped my fingers.

A club chair arose from the floor. I fell back into it, and kicked my feet up on the ottoman that appeared in front of me. As I dug through the couch cushion, a remote popped out. Pressing the power button, a TV appeared in front of me, and started playing cartoons, like *Elmo's World* and *Tom and Jerry*. Flipping through the channels, I found my favorite station. It showed a video of a finely dressed woman, in her mid-forties, sitting across a metal table.

"Okay Lib, I'm just going to ask you a few questions, okay, and I need you to answer them honestly. Okay? Great." She looked at the wall and nodded, then back toward the camera. "Question one – have you ever had suicidal thoughts?"

"No," a voice said, sounding defensive.

"Have ever had thoughts of harming another person?"

"No," the voice said.

"Have you ever had blackouts, or noticed any signs of amnesia or lost time?"

There was a short pause.

"Are we almost done?" the voice complained.

"Please answer the question," she calmly responded.

"Ugh ... No."

"The sooner you answer the questions, the sooner we can get you out of here. Now, have you ever blacked out, or noticed any signs of amnesia?" she asked again.

The voice was silent.

"Have you ever blacked out, or noticed any signs of amnesia?"

"You just said that." The voice now sounded irritated.

"Have you ever blacked out, or noticed any signs of amnesia?" once again, she asked.

"Stop it!" the voice said, getting aggressive.

"Have you ever blacked out, or noticed any signs of amnesia?"

"I already told you!" the voice barked.

It was quiet for a while, and then she asked once again, "Have you ever blacked out, or noticed any signs of amnesia?"

"Fuck you! Fuck this! I want to leave now!" The voice pounded his hand against the table.

"Have you ever blacked out, or noticed any signs of amnesia?"

"Let me out of here!" he screamed.

"Have you ever blacked out, or noticed any signs of amnesia?"

"Help! Help! Someone please help me!" The screen swung to the walls showing a one-way mirror. "Please anyone!" he banged on the glass.

"This will be a lot easier if you just answer the questions. Now if you please, have you ever blacked out, or noticed any signs of amnesia?" She asked once more.

He took a deep breath and returned to his seat.

The TV went blank. Looking back down at my hand, it was healed. Black sludge tears from my eyes, staining the chair. A box of tissues fell onto my lap. Using up half the box, I tossed them aside, then sat there in silence, not knowing what to do next.

A drink sounded nice. I placed a hand on the wall and a block pushed itself out, holding two glasses and a bottle of whiskey. Grabbing a glass and pressing it against the wall, two spherical ice cubes dropped into the cup. Most

29

people would call a bottle a party, I call it a starter. I poured the glass nearly full.

Sipping the drink, I walk back to the chair and snapped my fingers, molding it into one of those therapy couches. Lying back, finishing the whiskey, my eyes roll up to the ceiling.

"*Can I get you a refill, Sir?*" a butler said, appearing out of nowhere.

The butler was kind enough to pour me another glass.

All my life I have been forced to mingle with fools and dunces, watching them make poor decisions, one after the other. Whether it's drinking too much, sitting on their asses doing nothing, or just spending money as fast as a high school relationship.

The butler felt the need to add his two cents. "Sir, if you wish to converse, why not go and talk to your juvenile friend next door?"

"Sometimes words are better left unsaid."

"Sir, I am a figment of your imagination, the only reason I'm here is to amuse you."

The annoying thing was that he was right, but I won't give him the satisfaction.

"Well, you are doing a terrible job."

"Actually, it is you who are doing a terrible job, because, as I said ..."

"Leave." I waved him off.

"As you wish." The butler tiptoed backward, sinking into the wall.

The thought of my "juvenile friend next door" was troubling. If he wasn't part of me, would I have been able to stop that robber?

Whiskey was running low.

"Come on, don't lose sight of the truth. Remember, he is the villain. He's trying to get in your head." Advice from my reflection in the glass.

Gulping down the rest of the whiskey, I threw the glass at the wall, watching it shatter into dozens of pieces.

An alarm went off, and the room started to flood with water. In less than ten seconds, there was no air to breathe, choking on the water flooding my lungs. Everything became a red haze. My body felt helpless and my lungs burned. It was useless to fight. Everything comes to an end at one point or another. Why prolong the inevitable? The red turned to calming blackness.

I found myself hovering in a black void, bleak but calming. In the distance hovered my body, staring me down. I tried calling for it, but had no voice to speak with. It pointed to what seemed to be up. There was a light falling toward us. I could feel my skin peeling at the surface. The skin on my face tightened, as if being held back with hair clips. For the first time in decades I held a genuine smile, a real smile, making it feel all the scarier and more unnatural. The heat from the light was now causing my body to char and peel. Jaw bone could be seen peeking out of the corners; as I savored this moment, he did the strangest thing. My body waved to me as if saying hello for the first time.

Drenched in sweat and dripping drool, I was in need of the toilet. Getting out of bed was like getting out of a pool. Large droplets came off me, becoming stains on the carpet. Making my way toward the bathroom in the dark felt impossible, and everything felt out of place.

When I finally reached the bathroom, a gust of cold wind ran through me. Now freezing, on the verge of frostbite, I quickly found the light switch. The lights felt like the sun. Staggering toward the tub, I pulled on the hot water faucet to heat the room. A few minutes later, my eyes started to adjust. Finally, I was able to relieve myself and take a piss. The bottle of soap on the sink said "Succulent Honey." How many people have thought "Yeah, this will taste good"? Squeezing the bottle and turning on the sink faucet, I scrubbed all the grime out from under my fingernails. There was no hand towel next to the sink, as there usually was, so I just shook my hands dry. The water droplets splashed in my face, and I got soap water in my eyes. Leaning against the glass, my eyes started to water.

A burning old man slammed himself against the mirror, screaming, begging me to put him out of his misery.

Falling to the floor, I banged my head against the wall. It took a moment to pull myself together. Getting back up, I saw the mirror was now empty. Raising my eyebrows, opening my mouth, moving my head from side to side, still no difference. Telling myself it was just my imagination, I shut the light off, and worked my way back to what was now a water bed. Again, drenched in sweat, sleep was always a friend.

Deep breath in and out. In and out. In and out. This time I wasn't sinking, but just cold, as if chains were wrapped around my arms and legs, pulling them from their sockets. Skin stretched and torn. My knees and joints popped. A knife ran across my abdomen, opening up my chest cavity, scooping out my insides, leaving nothing but an empty pouch. As an empty carcass, though, I could feel my heart still pounding. Slowly, it started to dissipate. Each second the pounding got quieter, until there was nothing left. The pressure disappeared.

I opened my eyes to find myself in the room again, with him.

"How was the quarrel with the ghost, heard you took quite the fall?" he said, crouched in the corner, sounding slightly worried in his own monotonic way.

"Why do you care?" I said, rubbing my head.

"I may not have control, but this is my body too, and I would prefer that we not bleed out on the ground because of your carelessness."

"You're one to talk."

"And how many times did we come out on top? Lib, you need to understand that what I did, I did for us. To protect us."

"Don't! Don't you ... all that you have done is play mind games, and hurt others!" I snapped.

"It baffles me how naïve you can be," he said, turning to face me, the darkness covering his facial features.

"For a split second, I actually thought that maybe, just maybe, you did help stop the robbery. That maybe you changed for the better, but then I'm reminded of this anger inside of me. The type that claws at the back of my skull, telling me to keep hitting him. You make me become this monster that I can't control."

He mumbled something.

"What did you say?"

"And without that hate, you wouldn't have been strong enough to hold yourself back from killing that man."

Neither of us spoke.

The room started to shake, and then a crack opened and split the room in two. As his side sank, mine rose. A loud booming bounced off the wall, sounded so familiar. The pitch was getting higher the faster I ascended. It sounded like a school fire alarm ... My alarm clock is screaming at me.

Why do I have to leave so soon? I just barely got here.

The floor felt like a rocket leaving for space. In the distance was a speck, and as I got closer, I could make out letters spelling "E X I S T E N C E."

I braced myself for my own personal hell – reality.

3: The Best Drink Is Alone

PLEASE GOD, DON'T MAKE ME GET UP. Don't make me get up. The alarm decided not to be my friend, screaming in my ear.

Thanks.

Eyes still closed, slammed the snooze button.

"Good morning sunshine," It grunted.

"Muh." I groaned.

Just get up. Get up. At least move a toe.

It took about ten minutes to get out of the sweat-soaked mattress, wait no, the clock said thirty.

Taking one step felt like climbing a mountain.

I brushed the back of my tongue, causing me to gag several times over. Spit and rinse.

The water was freezing cold. Maybe splashing it in my face will wake me up. Nope. Just made me dread the day even more. As the droplets of water pitter-patter down the drain, I saw my reflection was somewhat fascinating. Seeing my eyes in the reflection having its own reflection. An ongoing cycle. It hurt to think about.

Taking a step back, popping my neck, something felt off, but I didn't see the point in looking for the answer. Now getting a wider angle, there seemed to be a lot of toothpaste back splash on the mirror. Using my thumb, I wiped it away, leaving behind smudges. It's going to take forever to get that marking out. The cheap spray will only make it worse. And rags, the wrong type of cloth, water marks are more frustrating than a tick buried under the skin. This whole thing has become a tremendous mess. The bed was not too far. Maybe God will take pity on me. Who am I kidding? He won't listen to me. All he does is stand up there and laugh at all of us. If you're listening, God, I hope you're happy.

Getting back to reality, I undressed myself, and worked up to getting in the shower. Too much strain. Still naked, it was time for breakfast. Looking through the cupboards and fridge, the best option was an egg over easy, on top of wheat toast, with a blended malt.

Getting a pan out, lathering it in olive oil, the bread started its process of tanning. The eggshell made a loud crack, similar to the sound of bones breaking. As it cooked in the pan, the toast popped. Fascinating, seeing how clear goo turns white as heat is applied. The spatula dove under, sweeping the miscarriage off its feet, flipping it over its back. There was a slight crackle, as if the yolk was screaming. The sound soon died off, and breakfast was nearly ready. Grabbing a plate, the toast made itself at home, its new roommate came in from behind and roughhoused with him a little. Grabbing some floozy out of the fridge, I looked through the glass apparel to see what she would look good in. The classical smooth cylinder always fancied my taste. A few cubes from the freezer would cool her off, making sure she wouldn't become distasteful.

Taking a seat at the kitchen table, the chair felt cold against bare skin. The first bite, bits of crumb fell to the floor and onto my lap. Toast never was a good bachelor. He always needed someone to stay satisfied. Second bite, egg revealed his heart to me, and I sucked him dry. Malt looked lonely over in the corner. Taking a sip of her helped move everyone's tastes around. The same newspaper was on the counter. Flipping to a new section, one headline wondered "What if JFK Was Still Alive?" It talked about Vietnam and how some historians make accusations on how the president would have confronted the issues. Unappetizing, reading how people say they know how an individual would act. As if to say they knew him for who he really was, or that he had no say in the dilemma.

After breakfast, the dishes cleaned, the attire awaited.

Color. Blue? Black? Gray? Brown? Squished between a red infused dark soot brown and gray lining bronze was a fawn tan blazer. A cotton white button-down was added into the mixture. A pair of black pleated pants truly made the ensemble come together, but what made jaws drop were the derby oil black shoes. Walking around in these makes the next guy over look like a putz. This was nice, like a glass being half full. Two steps forward. Three steps back.

The shoes made a classy sound with each step. It almost makes me want to dance. Seeing the blazer on my shoulders, giving me the power to bring someone to their knees with a single snap, marvelous. The button-down shirt, snug enough to show off some muscle tone, but not too much to where it looks paunchy. The pants themselves hide any and all insecurities under the belt, not too big, not too small, referring to the gluteus maximus, of course.

My phone went off, reminding me that reality awaits. The screen said "Text from Starbucks." Linda. The message read "Good Morning!" Meh. Mind your own business. No one wants to hear your happy-go-lucky voice in their head.

I whispered to myself, texting back, "Sorry, not feeling good. Can't make it in today."

Immediately she responded back. "OH NO! FEEL BETTER!!!"

Now that the day is mine, and the world is my rotten oyster.

"I see you're taking my advice. May I suggest you use some of that money from that shit job of yours, and pay a couple of hookers for an hour or two. Maybe rough them up, slit their throats, dance with the corpses a little."

I stayed quiet, acting as if I were actually considering the thought. "Hard pass." The time was a quarter past ten, and the buzz was wearing off. "How about a drink?"

Plugging in my earbuds, the journey to the bottom of a bottle commenced. Getting in my car, I drove to the nearest bar, a twenty-minute drive, plus five more to find a spot in the parking garage, extra ten to walk there. Standing outside the door, I removed my ear buds.

The bar was not the best looking, but I came here because I knew it would be empty. The booths were the classic red leather cushions, with a wooden underlayer. A jukebox stood against the wall, playing smooth jazz. Scratches covered the old wooden floor. Nails were poking out of the boards, waiting to be stepped on, and several vomit stains could be seen on the pool table. The whole room reeked of stale beer and stale smoke, but the smell was familiar and almost a comfort. As I took a seat at a bar stool, the bartender asked me what I wanted to drink.

I placed two hundred dollars on the bar. "One hour."

"Sorry buddy, but I'm not gonna just ..." I placed another two hundred on the bar. He took the money, then attempted a threatening look. "You break anything, I have your face on camera" and he went out the back.

On the other side of the bar, there was a small selection to choose from. A cocktail shaker stood by the ice under the bar. I grabbed a bottle of vodka, peach schnapps, an orange slice, and cranberry juice. I mixed together about six ounces of vodka, one ounce of the schnapps, three ounces of cranberry, and juice from the orange slice. I added one scoop of ice and placed the lid over the shaker. With one hand, I shook to the best of my ability, and with the other hand I reached for a tall glass. I poured and realized it looked like a blood-infused slushy. One sip, and it was quite clear that there was no blood in the drink. The bar stool was quite comfortable. Smooth jazz was nice to listen to, but it wasn't exactly to my taste. The cord stuck out from the side of the jukebox, plugged into the wall. Unplugging it wouldn't be a bad idea, but for now the background tune was nice.

The reach-in behind the bar made a small hum, showing off its one variety of beer. Drinking farther down the glass, the taste of the vodka was fading and the slush-ified ice was an interesting sensation – it started to numb my tongue, making me lose my sense of taste. Another minute went by, and my brain started to feel a bit warm. The sensation wasn't strong enough to block out the pain, but it was a start.

I grabbed another glass, and mixed four shots of whiskey with Diet Coke from the gun. Out of all the drinks I've ever had, out of all the margaritas and mimosas and other cocktails, Diet Coke and whiskey are the perfect match. Never have I met another mixture where you can't taste the alcohol. This drink can only be brought out on special occasions.

Today is the anniversary of the day when my life went to shit. The day that got me thrown into a hole, filled with the delusional. Seeing the look on everyone's faces, as if I am a monster. Maybe I am. I was there. I was the one standing in the blood at the end of it all.

"Fun times to come." I could feel Its grimacing smile clawing at the back of my skull.

His voice brought only pain, and luckily my medicine was right in front of me.

"Will anyone else be joining this party?"

I licked my lips several times as I replied. "Well, I was hoping to be by myself, but that's obviously not going to happen."

"And sometimes it's better to be with the ones you love. Lucky for both of us."

As I finished off the drink, his intolerable voice started to sound almost bearable. "Go fuck yourself," I said, in a calming manner. "When the day comes, when my dream comes true, you will be the one who has everything to lose, and I'll be halfway to heaven or hell."

It ignored my second bit of commentary. "You know, I would, but I don't seem to have any hands. Maybe you can help with that?"

Time for another drink. This time something a bit stronger, to take off the edge quickly. A shot of fireball. It was always interesting to down a shot of fireball, making my breath smell like cinnamon, as if I had just come from the apple pie baking contest, where the old grandma always seems to come first each year, and all the other contestants are thinking she's a bitch for it.

I rubbed my lips to see if any drool came out. Nope. Just my words.

"How does it feel to put yourself in such a vulnerable state?" it said, sounding pesty.

"If you could see my mouth, it would say I don't care."

I walked over to the pool table, swaying a bit on the way over.

Pool sticks make a good third leg. I racked up the balls and broke, and the game was afoot.

"Dibs on stripes."

"Eh, it doesn't matter if you're playing for me. Stripes are for losers anyway."

There was a clear shot of the 9 ball across the table. Miss and a scratch.

"Wow, what an amazing shot. Three red, top right corner, bounce off the wall."

Sunk.

"Well ... this is fun."

Huffing, I went to get another drink. A tall bottle of red wine stood on a little shelf on the wall. It looked like a prized possession, something the owner took pride in. Maybe it was the first bottle he'd ordered. Maybe it was the bottle he was going to share with his dead wife. Doesn't matter, soon enough I'll be drowning myself in it. There was no corkscrew to be seen, but I did spot a little crème brûlée torch. Using the flame, I heated the neck of the bottle. Slowly, the cork rose from its chambers, then popped. No need to waste another glass; the bottle will do just fine.

"Whose – ah – whose turn is it?" as I swigged on the bottle.

"Mine. Green six hits one yellow, both in middle left."

"Risky business."

"Hit the ball already."

They sank.

"How's it feel to get your ass kicked by yourself?"

His annoying grunt was starting to get on my nerves.

"Red seven, top left."

Aiming carefully, I did a few air taps. I lined up for the shot, seeing the straight shot, only four feet from me. I shot the pool stick forward, aiming too high, causing the stick to scrape the top of the cue ball.

"Oh, damn it. I guess it's my turn," sounding unapologetically sarcastic.

Blue number twelve was begging me to sink it, standing only a few inches from the bottom left corner pocket. Lining up for the shot, I could see the winning cup, that being the bottom of this shitty wine. One drink for good luck. The pool stick bang-scraped the bottom of the table, causing the ball to leap across the room, smashing into a picture on the wall. Glass fell to the floor as the ball followed behind, leaving the shattered carnage of what looked to be an old family photo.

"Magnificent," It said, now sounding sarcastic. "May I suggest ..."

"Shut up." Frustrated, I scratched again.

"All I was going to say ..."

"Pick a fucking ball." I was feeling the pool stick starting to crack.

It took an unnecessary breath. "All right, bounce off the back wall, hitting blue two, sinks in top right corner."

I wasn't that good a shot.

The ball ran across the table, bounced off the wall, and I was hearing the loud clack and watching as all my sanity jumped out the window.

"No, no, no, no, no, no, no! Stop! Fuh!" I took a few deep breaths. "Okay ... No, no, no. It's my turn now. I don't care about your turn, because it should be mine! My fucking turn!"

I lined up for orange thirteen, straight shot to the bottom right corner pocket, and I took a few deep breaths, trying to get a grip. I closed my eyes and relaxed my hands, feeling the pool stick run through my fingers like butter on a sunny day. Envisioning the ball falling into its pocket, letting me find the slightest bit of decency in this rigged game. Deep breath in. The stick comes back. Exhale.

My phone goes off.

The white shitball took a curve right, hitting the eight ball instead.

"Well, how's that for luck?"

No words could describe my anger at this moment. The phone was still ringing, waiting to be answered. After a while, it went to voicemail. The room was silent. He didn't dare to say a word. This piece of garbage. I smashed the stick against the table, snapping off the top piece.

The phone went off again.

Pulling myself together, I answered. "What?" I brushed my hair back.

"Dude! We got the job."

"Job? Who is this?"

"Phil, man! Dude! We're getting our own branches! We're managers, man!

"Oh, cool. Um ... do I need to come to the office, or ... um?" trying to calm down.

"Dude, how are you not excited right now?"

"I-I am, I'm just processing it all. Hey, I got to go."

"Okay dude, but get down here! Our offices are sweet!"

I disconnected the call.

"Best two out of three?"

Something fell on my shirt. Drool was dripping from my lower lip at a steady stream. Wiping it away, my hand felt disgusting. There was a little sink behind the bar. A brown sludge dripped out when I turned on the faucet. Vodka would have to do as a temporary, using my hair as a paper towel. I headed for the door.

It was too bright outside; my eyes felt like they were going to melt. Taking one step in front of the other wasn't such a cakewalk either. Every few steps, I would stumble a bit, nearly falling on my face. The spinning was a good distraction from the vomit wanting to crawl up my throat. Breathing was odd. Taking in oxygen, carbon, nitrogen, and evaporated piss smell of the street. Sweat was pouring down my center like a rainstorm, ruining my feng shui. Tiny droplets of sweat fell from my face onto my exemplary shirt. *Unacceptable*, I thought, bacteria will flood the fabric, causing it to rot from the inside out. In less than three hours, if it is not cleaned, the rot will be irreversible. Imagining the yellow grime was sickening enough.

I could see a convenience store about a block up. It's unlikely, I thought, but if they have any stain cleaner, maybe life is worth living. I walked in and noticed that the store smelled as if the floors were cleaned with vinegar and cat pee. There was a small section of cleaning supplies along the wall to my right. Brushes and sponges dangled from the hooks, with dish soap standing under them, but no stain removal product. Wow, someone's really looking out for me up there.

Overall the store looked like a piece of garbage. Candy wrappers and empty beer cans covered the floor. Chewed-up gum was stuck to the display coolers. The ceiling had large holes in it, with a combination of yellow and black staining. A bottle of antifreeze was spilled in the next aisle over, and I was half certain I saw a raccoon in the adjacent room where they store all the refrigerated beer. My head started to lose that warm fuzzy feeling, and I decided the risk was worth it. Grabbing a hammer and a chamois rag off a shelf, I opened the door to the liquor room, and it was bleak. All they had was canned beer and gin – everything else looked to have already been bought or stolen. One bottle should be sufficient, though.

I turned around with it, and something ran past my leg and out the front doors. Fun. My stomach was growling. Something to snack on maybe? The snack section was depressing: generic cheesy puffs, a box with a frog holding a churro ... but at least they have Double Stuff Oreos. The one good thing in this store that probably hasn't been poisoned or got some kind of body fluid on it. No one was at the counter, but it did have a bell that said ring me. I did. Shuffling could be heard from the back, but no greeting. Again, I rang the bell, but only briefly.

"Hold on!" someone yelled from the back.

A few minutes passed by, and still no one came out. This was ridiculous. Making my way toward the exit, a voice hollered, "You need to pay for that!"

Turning around, I saw that the man standing behind the counter looked like an average self-indulgent person.

The first thing that caught my attention was his face. His beak of a nose was bruised, possibly broken, and veering to the left. The eyes had sunk deep into his skull, causing large bags to form underneath. His face was covered in tiny scars and scabs. He looked more closely related to a skeleton than any living thing I've ever encountered. The truly odd feature was the lack of eyebrows and burnt hair.

The fashion statement was "Ten months unwashed and counting." The baggy short-sleeve shirt was covered in holes, and the blue jeans looked more like brown jeans.

"Y-y-you need to pay for that," he said, sounding jittery, scratching his face.

"Oh yeah, sorry." I walked back over to the counter.

Getting a closer look, I saw his eyes were bloodshot, giving him a sort of murderous vibe.

He started clicking on the keyboard. The computer made a few beeps, as if they were communicating. There was a long back and forth with him and the computer and he made a few chuckles, running his fingers across the screen as if he were shushing it.

"Oh you." The guy let out a belly laugh, fell to the floor, and lay there not making a sound.

Confused by this, I rang the bell.

"Hello?"

The freak jumped to his feet. "How can I help you?" with a hideous smile.

The one tooth glued to the front of his rotting gums looked more like a toothpick.

"That will be two billion dollars."

"Oh, a little pricey there, any chance you can get me a discount on those Oreos?"

"Yep ... that will be $3.78."

"Mhmm, still costly. But okay." I handed him a five. "Keep the change."

"Sweet!" he said.

I made my way to the exit and the guy shouted at me, "Come back soon! Sullivan's Station, your next stop." The unhinged smile leaked brown liquid from his gums like snoose.

Walking out of the store, it burned my throat to take in the fresh air. It took me a couple of seconds, but I was able to open the bottle. The street was filled with ugly people smiling at one another. Gin was the only honest person on the sidewalk. Gin doesn't tell lies, not at 40 percent alcohol. Yep, definitely not a lie. My goal was to finish half the bottle before I got to work. No more pit stops, no breaks to catch my breath. That feeling of despair, hating my life, and everything in it needed to go numb. Breathing didn't feel like such a bother. The beggars on the street didn't smell like 5-day old under-the-sun piss. Putting one foot in front of the other was a bit challenging, but if everything was easy then the world would be filled with golden-age geniuses, and most likely nothing would get done. Half the world would be starving, while the other half would be enlarging.

A little girl in a pink dress and ribbons was skipping down the street, no care in the world. Just wait, I thought, it will find a way to fuck you over, and if it doesn't then everyone will resent you for it.

I might as well end it all now – let Death know I'm hoping to meet him soon. I don't want to be an inconvenience when I die. Some random stranger finds me on the floor of my home and is then scarred for life. No. Jumping off a building would be too messy a waste of time for the police. No. Drowning myself would be interesting, but I've heard it can be quite uncomfortable, so no. Swallowing a pistol muzzle and eating a bullet – probably the best way to go, but can't be in some confined space. Too risky. Bullet could go through the wall and kill some annoying rosy-cheeked dreamer. That wouldn't be fair to them.

Great, I'm at the front door of the building where I work, and I've finished only a third of the liter bottle of gin. As usual I can't do anything right. Clap. Go ahead. Clap for the person who can't do anything right. Thank you. Oh, you're so kind. What an honor it has been to hate you all. To my mother, who doesn't see me for who I am, and my late father, taken too soon from this fine world. The only man who knew right from wrong. I have one thing to say, and one thing only, and that is ... I hope you all burn in hell. Yes. Thank you. Thank you. You're too kind. Hold the applause.

I handed the gin bottle to some sad sap on his way out the door, spreading my joy. On my way in, I happened to notice two security guards carrying an upside-down Bennett out by his wrists and ankles. He howled, begging them to give him another chance. Unfortunately he spotted me.

"Lib! Lib! Tell them what a great boss I am!"

The two security guys stopped, dangling Bennett's belly just inches off the ground.

This opportunity was most definitely not an occasion that I could pass up. On the one hand, the high road, telling the guards how this crying fool was good at his job, making him look like a star, just really didn't feel good. I'd much rather tell them about how this thing dangling in front of me was more animal than human, always wanting to stick his dick into any hole he could fit it in. Yet, seeing the tears roll down his face was hard to look at. It made him look like a naked squirrel.

"He is single-handedly the most perverted, fucked-up, repulsive man I have ever known," I told them. "He has continuously harassed women – and men – around the office. This man should be where he belongs – in the garbage with the rest of the trash."

"You motherfucker!" he shrieked. "I'll kill you! I'll slit your throat in your sleep, and feed you to my fucking dog!"

He screamed this and other things on his way out, but I didn't care enough to listen much more.

"Guarantee, in a week's time, he'll be selling himself in Vegas for five dollars," It said, sounding certain.

The elevator doors opened and I noticed again that the canned music sounded like something from a 1940s movie. As the doors closed, I pushed the 58 floor button. As the cab rose though, my stomach sank. My internal organs felt like they'd been stirred in a pot. My legs went numb, and the spinning didn't feel very good. I crumpled to the floor, and everything went dark.

As I slowly came around, I found myself lying in the dark, covered in dirt and dead leaves. It smelled musty and fervid and rank with rot. A whistle echoed, not that far away, and I began to feel like a wounded animal. Struggling to my feet, I noticed a shadowy figure off in the distance. I stared at it – and it stared back – for the longest time. I could feel its anger, and the pain that came with it.

Finally it waved its hand in the air – like it was saying hello. I dared not reciprocate. The big shadow form started moving forward. And the whistling was getting louder. An icy chill shivered down my spine as the crunch of dead branches rang louder in my ear. I very slowly backpedaled to see what the response might be. The shadow then picked up its speed, shifting from a stalk to more of a trot.

I turned and started to jog, and became aware that the the whistling now was even louder than before. The ground beneath my feet was shaking, like I was running on a bed or a trampoline, almost as if it were going to break in half.

Then everything stopped. The crunching. The whistling. The shaking. I turned around and the shadow behind me had coalesced into a man – sort of – who now stood just ten feet from me. It was too dark to make out a face, but what stood there looked more beast than human – about eight feet tall and three feet wide. Enormous claws on the ends of grizzly-size paws, with dark blackish fur over most of its body. Upright like a sasquatch, perhaps, yet not imaginary.

My heart was racing, pounding out of my chest, and I could hear it in my ears, yet I couldn't move. No matter how much I struggled, my body was like stone. We locked eyes with one another. My mind went completely blank and instantly everything was completely okay.

It doesn't matter. It never did.

I closed my eyes and calmly waited. The beast or whatever it was rushed me, I heard the grunt as it swiped claws across my face.

I was back on the floor of the elevator, slowly coming to, still crumpled on the floor. Alone. I focused on the ding as it stopped on my floor, and I

53

unhappily noticed the vomit covering the floor. Had to be mine. The doors slid open, and a cluster of people stood silently looking at me.

Sweat dripped down my face and ribs as I struggled to my feet. The people in the hallway looked at me with shock and disgust.

"Sorry."

They all stepped aside hurriedly, edging away so I didn't touch them. Phil was there, talking to one of our new co-workers, and he saw me.

He stepped nearer. "Bro, you don't look so good."

"Really," I glared at him, "I feel great." I wanted to break his jaw but I barely had the energy to even make that comment in his direction.

"Let me show you around," he said. He aggressively took my elbow and piloted me away from the others, away from the stinky elevator.

"So, over here is the employee lounge," he told me. "Through those doors over there is the conference room. To our left, our offices, and you have Bennett's old office. He didn't leave peacefully, if you know what I mean."

"Yeah," I glanced at Phil, "we talked on his way out."

"Oh cool, you know then." He slapped me on the back. "Eww, gross!" he recoiled a bit. "Why are you all sweaty?" Apparently he hadn't seen me lying down in the puke in the elevator. I'd had enough if his cheerleading and headed off to take a nap in my new office. The door glass still said H. Bennett. "They'll get that fixed by tomorrow," Phil said helpfully.

I shoved open the door and saw all his stuff was still on the desk. A fairly stylish leather couch sat over to the right, waving at me. I dove into it and fell back into the cushions and closed my eyes.

"Hey bro." He was still there.

"You're still here?" I asked.

"Okay, so there's this party downtown tonight, and I heard there's going to be some really hot babes. So I was thinking you could be my wingman."

"Fine. Just get the fuck out."

"Sweet. I'll text you the address." I heard the door close behind him.

Falling from the Strings

4: Our Past Defines Us

THE LUCID ROOM WAS MADE OUT OF ANGER, to lock away the desecrator, to keep me sane. The irony of all this dismay is that I am the one who feels confined to a meaningless story, while he crouches in the corner, silently mocking me.

"How's the darkness, cold and bleak I hope?"

The smooth cool marble wall felt almost soothing. Life shouldn't (and never will) be a place to find conventional standards, because if you blink everything you care for is gone.

"If you're done reminiscing over my benevolence, I'd like to talk."

I turned my head to look at him, and snapped my fingers. Two club chairs, on opposite sides of the room, molded themselves from the ground. I turned mine to face the dark side, and my friend did the same to face the light. We took our seats. The room was quiet, nice ... until he broke the silence.

"Haven't been in one of these in a while. You really do care for me. How sweet." He was sounding like his typical ill-mannered self.

I snapped my fingers, and his chair morphed into an old rickety chair, with nails sticking out of the seat.

"Quaint. So, rolling with the high rollers I see; must be fun picking up their spare change."

"Just means that I have more responsibility, fair salary, better than the next guy."

"With money, there is power, and power is what separates the weak from the strong," he said, sounding hard. "It reminds me of a quote once said by a wise man, 'Life should never be a place for aspiration to find conventional standards in the endless scenarios to be played out; it's always limited to a single ending ... carnage.'"

"Oh, and who said that?"

"Me."

He's ridiculous, trying to portray himself as something more than an ant under a boot. "For the past three years I was slumming with 'these animals.' What's with the all of a sudden burst of joy?"

"Just have a feeling about your new boss. She is different."

"And what's that supposed to mean?"

"I don't know. Just a feeling."

"Hmmmm." I slowly scratched my cheek, staring at him for the longest time. Neither of us spoke. Sometimes it felt like words were useless, like everything has been already said and done, yet here we still are, still standing.

"How do you do it?" deeply exhaling.

"Do what?"

"Look at me. Talk to me. Be in the same room with me. I locked you in this prison, and you still don't hate me."

"Believe me, I more than hated you when I was first trapped here. Then over time I came to realize that you were the only one who sees me for who I really am. Everyone thought I was you. So, what's the point of hating the only person who knows that I exist, the only person who knows the truth about me?" He was now shining his pearly white teeth at me.

"How sweet. Maybe next time we can dine on tea and cookies." I was *not* buying his sad story. "You know what I think, I think this whole nice guy act is just that, an act. Fake. You're just a runaway idea that went too far to control, and I hate myself for it. So, stop! Stop wearing this mask. Show yourself!"

"I tried to be nice, I tried to help you, and I tried to create a common ground. I have shown you countless times that I have changed. I showed you the truth."

"I-I-I-I-I-I-I-I! Shut up!"

"You think that I'm the reason you live such a shit life? That's on you. We could be kings – even friends – by now, but you won't give me a chance to prove myself."

"Fuck you, and fuck your dream too!"

I stood up and snapped my fingers. The chairs vanished and my friend fell to the floor. I snapped my fingers once more, and chains wrapped around his body. This forced him into a mummified position, levitating him off the floor. Once more, I snapped my fingers, and the chains brought him past the darkness, over next to me.

"What are you doing? Let me go!"

"You think you're so pure, well, let me show you how you just altogether fuck my life up." I covered his mouth with my hand.

My friend tried to speak but all that came out was some muffled umphs.

"Ah, ah, ah. No talking." I released my hand from his face, only to find that his mouth was gone.

I turned around and placed my hands on the wall. The room started to flicker and turn a deep blood red color.

Without saying another word, we began our journey down a long hallway. There were doors, some with labels like the *rooftop* or *prison for the fallen demon*. Paintings covered the walls, one showing a young boy sitting at a table, staring at a revolver with a bullet laid next to it. At the end of the hallway was an old beaten-up door labeled "*The Beginning.*"

"Why don't we peek inside, and see what hides behind this door."

Turning the door handle, a loud creak echoed around us. Toys and crayons were scattered across the floor. The only light source was from the holes on the walls. In the small dark corner was a young boy crying into his pillow. He couldn't have been older than five or six. Screaming could be heard off in the background – a man and a woman. Glass was being shattered; holes were made. We walked nearer toward the child, getting in close. Being very quiet, the boy was trying hard to hold back his tears, squeezing his raggedy teddy bear, which looked both burnt and cut. It was missing an eye and one of its feet.

"We need to go," the teddy bear said in a soft voice.

"No, w-we need to stay," whimpered the boy. "Nobody wants us."

"We don't belong here."

There was a loud thud, and they were both startled as a meat tenderizer busted another hole in the wall.

"I think we've heard enough," I said, and I left the room.

We found our way back into the hallway to search for a new door. My friend motioned at me, wanting to speak again. I snap my fingers and his lips re-emerge.

"This won't change anything. You can't change the past."

I decided to ignore him, and find a new door on my own.

"Oh, this one should be good." The door was made of a red plastic, and instead of a door knob, there was a yellow pirate steering wheel. On top of it was a label that said "*Play Time.*"

This time we just barged right on in. We were at my old elementary school playground. There was the same boy, same as the last door, but now a few years older. He sat still on a swing reading a book.

As he flipped through the pages, another boy swaggered up to him.

"Hey, what are you reading, must be something stupid like what president was the smartest dumbo?"

"You're a dumbo," muttered the boy on the swing, barely giving the bully any notice.

"You are such a nerd."

"He's just saying that, because he's the butthole," a mouthless voice said.

"Just go away," the swing boy complained.

"Oh, you gonna cry," taunted the bully. Wawawawa!"

"Don't say anything," the voice slowly cautioned.

"I'm not," mumbled the boy.

"Yes you are," the bully said, and he shoved the boy off the swing.

"Stop! Knock it off!" the boy whined. He struggled to his feet.

"Or what?" the bully continued to push him.

"Stop!" he screamed.

"Make me!" the bully taunted back, shoving him back onto the ground.

"Let me help you," gently said the voice.

"Go away!" the boy cried.

"Come on, get up wimp!" the bully laughed, throwing rocks at him.

"Let me in!" the voice demanded.

"No!" the boy yelled back.

"You're just a stupid little idiot!" the bully said, now kicking rocks at him.

The boy let out a wailing cry.

"Say it!" barked the bully, kicking rocks and dirt.

The boy stayed curled up on the ground, doing nothing, barely whining. The bully kept kicking and kicking until he got tired.

"What, got nothing to say?" he demanded, nudging the boy with a shoe in the back.

No response.

"Stop crying, you crybaby!"

Still no response.

The bully nudged him some more. He grabbed the boy's shoulder to turn him over. Suddenly the boy pounced off the ground and leaped swiftly onto the bully. He shoved him to the ground, flinging his fists in every direction. The bully tried to stop him, but all he could do was squirm.

He kept hitting him even after his hands started to ache. It wasn't until a playground helper ran over to pry him from the bully that he finally stopped. I got a look at the bully then, just to see the damage. He had a bloody nose, and there was a deep cut across his forehead. His cheeks were flushed, but his eyes started to turn purple, his left eye starting to show hemorrhage.

"What did you do?" the boy asked, shying from what he was looking at.

"I stopped him," the voice said, sounding satisfied.

It was almost impossible to detect, but a tiny smile was perched on the corner of the boy's mouth.

"Why are we here, Lib? What's the point of all of this? You want me to apologize for what I've done! Fuck you if you think that's happening," It struggled, trying to get free of the chains.

"I want you to disappear. But you ... you are my eternal nightmare."

"And my being locked up these past years doesn't compare?"

"Not in the slightest." I was getting uncomfortably close to his face.

"Well, I assume there's another door to be entered. So get on with it already."

I snapped my fingers and stomped back into the hallway. This was indeed a special door. There was no door handle, no automated open and close feature; this was a door you had to knock on and wait for someone to invite you in. Only then would it open.

A hysterical voice from inside called come in, and the door swung open. The room had a glossy white marble look, and the only thing inside was a bed with straps on it. A nurse came from behind me and walked right through me.

"It's time to take your medicine," the nurse said, and she handed the young man a cup of water and a pill.

"Okydoky." He grabbed the pill and then proceeded to put the pill on his tongue and drink the water. He stuck out his tongue to show the nurse he'd swallowed it, and drooled a little in the process.

"Great job, since you've been such a good boy, I got you a pudding cup from the cafeteria."

The young man snatched the pudding cup and tore it open. As the nurse left and reached back to shut the door behind her, the young man gave her a huge smile with his tongue sticking out, showing the pudding he was about to swallow. When she walked away, he immediately changed his posture. He stood right up, wiped away the puddling smeared on his face, and started to pace back and forth. While pacing, he spat out the pill that was tucked under his tongue. It fell to the floor, and he crushed it into powder with a twisting of his shoe.

He started to mumble something under his breath, then frantically leaped onto his bed and began jumping up and down.

"No!" he shouted, jumping off the bed and slamming against the wall.

Picking himself up from the floor, he dashed to the door and held his right ear on it, trying to listen in on what was happening on the other side. A thud could be heard getting louder, getting closer each second with his ear held on the door. Eyes widened and he hurtled into the corner of the room, his face tucked into his shirt. The door crashed open and a very large man stepped in. He looked to be in his late forties, bald, wearing a lab coat.

"How's my favorite patient doing today?" his voice rose up and back in intensity.

The young man didn't respond.

"Are you there ... is there meat in that dumpling? Hello?" He waved his hands and snapped his fingers at the boy.

Pulling a scalpel from his pocket, the doctor placed it lightly against the young man's forehead. "I have been very patient with you these past few weeks. Now either you let me see him, or you will be dissected, and you'll be nothing more than just pieces for scientists to examine," the doctor whispered in his ear.

Nothing.

"Have it your way." The doctor started to slice across the back of my head. Before he was a centimeter deep, the boy grabbed the doctor's arm with his left hand, and with his right hand free, he shattered the doctor's nose. Blood gushed out like a spigot, making a small depression between his eyes. The man fell back, and the boy didn't waste a second to pounce and pound on him. He threw his fist right into the doctor's liver, and could feel the ribs break like peanut shells. A foot spiked into the doctor's testicles, causing him to uncontrollably shit himself and vomit onto the floor.

The boy decided to take a break from beating on the doctor, and he grabbed his pudding cup. He scraped what was left out of it and then scooped up vomit. He poured it back into the doctor's mouth, and the doc gagged and tried to spit it out, but was forced to swallow it by having his nostrils closed off. Struggling to find the power to swallow, the doctor choked down his food for a second time.

Unfortunately for the boy, at this moment the door banged open and two large men grabbed him and forced him against the wall. Right behind the men came a nurse wielding a syringe filled with a clear liquid. The boy struggled, tossing and turning, but escape was not an option. He kicked the air in front of him to keep the nurse away, but was shoved to the floor so the big guys could lock his knees in place. The needle point looked as if it were the size of a screwdriver. Proceeding cautiously, the nurse moved in, crouched down, and pierced his neck.

As she pressed on the syringe, the boy started to calm down. He moved slowly, so slowly that it was like watching a snail moving against the wind. My eyes drifted away from the boy, and everything else seemed to be in slow motion as well. The nurse was pulling the needle out of his neck like a sloth, and the two men were floating a few inches off the ground, trying to leap backward. The room started to become blurry, but it was not my eyes that deceived me, the room itself and the contents inside of it, including the people, did start to become obscured, turning into a massive curtained blur. The room got darker, slowly, until it was pitch black. The door behind us opened, though, and we left.

"Thank you for the trip down memory lane, but if this was some kind of scheme to make me feel a deep sorrow, then you have failed. I am satisfied."

I didn't say anything, instead giving him a pensive look.

"What, cat got your tongue? You brought me here and now you won't speak. This is turning out to be quite the show. Someone quick, get me some popcorn!"

"I give up. I can't save you."

"I don't need to be saved. You and all the other animals don't understand. Life is just a façade ready to punch you in the face. You'll see, the brave will fall and the cowards will survive. The modern world is just so – what's the word – *humdrum*. Look at the Spartans, the most badass civilization to have ever lived. They tossed the weak aside to die, so the strong could live. Today's society is just a bunch of alarmists hiding behind their little screens. You want to know why I hate society – you should really be asking why society is fucking itself over so badly."

I ran my fingers across the chains. The freezing metal caused my fingers to go numb. I'm befuddled, not knowing what to do or say, I kept running my hands across the icy restraints. He's a monster who wishes to be a kingpin in a world that would burn under his reign. Maybe I'm doing this wrong. Maybe to control this thing, I need to see his perspective.

I snapped my fingers, and an axe grew from the ground. With my left hand I grasped the bottom of the wooden handle, then I set my right closer to the blade.

Sounding confused and distressed he asked, "What are you doing?" as It tried to break free from the chains.

Bracing my feet in a sturdy position to get leverage, I slowly moved the axe back and forth against his head.

"Lib, this isn't funny!"

"When did I ever aspire to being a comedian?"

I brought the axe back over my shoulder and swung it over, aiming for his thick skull. I swung so hard that I could feel the handle cracking as it crashed, and it nearly split his head in two. The axe became lodged, and as I tried to haul it out, blood drained down onto the floor. Finally, the axe was free from the binding skull. There wasn't enough carnage, so I switched the axe over to its butt and swung again. Blood splattered on the walls, on the ceiling, on my face. It tasted of wine. Each swing brought me an arousing joy. By the time I was finished, the only thing left was a pool of red and bits of skull scattered across the floor. Chunks of brain splattered in every crease and crevice.

I got on my knees. Placing my hands on the puddle, I pressed down. My hands started to sink. My elbows were soaked. Eventually, I was swimming in the fine wine. I dove down, and kept swimming until my lungs nearly burst, and then I swam some more. There was a lighter distance. I forced myself to paddle forward. Hitting the surface, I gasped for air.

Pulling myself up onto the cold dirt, I lay there on the ground to catch my breath. The air burned, making my lungs shrivel up and cramp. Pulling myself up off the ground, I looked around my surroundings. No hallways or doors now, just a dark gloomy abyss. The sky was empty. The ground, dirt. The only light was from the pedestals on my left with an array of weapons sitting atop them. Every weapon was different from the last: knives, guns, axes, whips, stethoscope, and so many others. Walking over to one of the pedestals, I saw it contained a pair of silver-plated brass knuckles.

They piqued my interest, so I grabbed them to take a closer look. Bringing them up to eye level, I could see my reflection. My eyes were swollen red. As I started to tear up, something moved in the reflection behind me. Without making any sudden movements, I slid the brass knuckles on and tucked my arms in, ready to fight. Turning around, I saw a skeleton of a man before me. He had no shirt on, showing his scars on his abdomen. His face looked disfigured and bludgeoned. He was a feeble-looking character, arms the size of toothpicks. He had a few inches on me, though, and was covered in dried-up dirt.

"Ah ... Hi?" I tried, not making any sudden movements.

There was a psychotic hunger in his emerald-shaded eyes. He engaged and put his fists up.

"Now hold on, this-"

He swung at me, and I ducked left. Pivoting left, I twisted my hips and threw a left hook hard into his ribcage. With him falling to the ground with his newly cracked ribs, I leaped backward.

"Listen to me," I said, keeping my voice in a calming monotone.

But the man got back up and proceeded to charge at me. Instead of standing still, like a normal person, I waited for the right moment and pivoted again, and this time I broke his jaw. He fell into the dirt, blood throbbed down his neck, mixing in with his drool. It seemed impossible but he was still conscious.

"Last chance, stay down."

He grumbled, scraped up dirt, and threw it into my eyes. My eyes burned. I tripped backward. While I tried to clear my eyes, a sharp pain hit my lower right abdomen. Following it came a blow to my head. I fell to the ground but quickly pulled myself back up. My eyes started to water. I felt helpless punching the air around me, hoping that I could land at least one punch. A sharp pain erupted from my liver. As I collapsed, he jumped on top of me, throwing punch after punch. I forced my hands to cover my face, hoping to block whatever he threw at me. Soon he was spent, and that was my chance to strike. Punching thin air repeatedly, I was able to land a single punch – to the throat. I could hear him gag. He fell over trying to breathe. I got the dirt out of my eyes, and I could see his face turning purple, his tongue thick as a baseball.

I caught my breath. "I told you to stop. Why didn't you listen?" I sat down next to him as he twitched and gargled. "Why couldn't you have just left me alone? Now you're suffocating. Fuck. Sometimes it just feels like there is no point in trying. Sometimes I-"

Looking down, I saw his eyes roll back in his head.

Water like mercury leaked from his mouth, creating a large puddle. Looking inside, I saw my ugly self. I dipped my finger in the water, and a ripple shivered across the whole puddle. My reflection disappeared and was replaced with a teenage boy walking down a hallway in a high school. He had his headphones covering his ears; he ignored his surroundings. Walking down the hallway he saw groups of people huddled together talking and laughing. No one seemed to notice they were bumping into a human being.

One tall teenage boy with dark green eyes came up to him and stopped him in his tracks.

The nuisance snagged the headphones off the boy's head. "Hey shit-for-brains, can anyone hear me in there?" He stood waving his hands in front of the boy's face.

"Yes, I can hear you. Give me back my headphones," the boy said, reaching to take them back.

"No, they're mine now!" The nuisance stood laughing at the boy's face.

The teenager made the mistake of pushing the tall nuisance, who then grabbed the boy by the collar and slammed him against the lockers.

The boy squirmed and squealed. "Stop it!"

"Just let go," a voice said.

"Come on, do something retard-ation," the bully laughed.

"Leave me alone!" he screeched.

Other students started to crowd around them.

"Look everybody, it's the freak without a brain! Watch as he squirms and screams when my hand touches his face." The nuisance licked his hand, rubbing it over the boy's face.

The boy did squirm and scream. No one stepped in. No one spoke up. Instead, there was laughter. The boy flailed one of his legs, kicking the bully where it hurt. He squalled and threw the boy back and forth against the lockers.

A teacher soon arrived, shouting, "Get out of the way!" to the students, but before he could reach us the bully let me go and stomped on my headphones. With a few seconds to spare, he ran off and was out of sight. By the time the teacher reached him, he was balled up on the floor, with fresh warm tears running down his face. To make matters worse, the teacher grabbed him by the arm and hauled him to the principal's office. The image transcended then to a classroom, full of miscreants. In the front left corner desk sat the same boy being picked on. He had his hands covering his ears, murmuring to himself.

The door swung open. The teacher marched in, slamming the door behind him.

"Everybody take a seat. You there, why are you here?" the teacher barked, pointing at the wannabe gangster.

"Because some fag snitched on me." He turned to fist-bump his wannabe gangster friends.

"Wrong, sir!" exclaimed the teacher. "You, the one who smells like mar-i-JEW-ana, why are you here?"

"Cause some of y'all don't understand that I wasn't smoking my blunt. I was just putting it against my lips."

Again, the teacher said "Wrong!" He looked disgusted. "I would keep asking why you are all here, but it's obvious that none of you delinquents understand the meaning of right and wrong. All of you are here because you do not believe the rules apply to you, or you think you are right just because it was funny. Let me tell you something. All of you are not good people. Good people don't get sent to detention. Good people get rewarded. Detention is here to rehabilitate you, and make you become better people. I'm not saying that you will ever be good people. Oh no. Detention will make you into moderate people. If it were up to me, all of you would getting an ass whuppin' right about now, but I don't make the rules. So sit down and shut up!" Nearly out of breath, he sagged back into his chair and resumed reading his newspaper.

The teenagers huddled in the back were all whispering to each other. Every few minutes the teacher would look up from his newspaper and give them a riveting stare. They would be silent for a few seconds, and then continue on as if nothing had happened. Eventually they got bored with talking and started shooting spit wads. Crumpling up their shredded homework in teeny pieces and soaking it in their saliva, they shot at "the innocent." At first he tried to ignore them, but that was hopeless. Then he politely asked them to stop.

"Can you please stop being the blockheaded assholes you are and just quit?" Apparently, the request was far too complicated for the neanderthals to understand. It was less than a minute later they started up again.

Everything went slowly fuzzy on him. Screaming out of frustration, he grabbed a nearby desk and heaved it at them. Luckily for him, two of the apes didn't move fast enough, and had their heads smashed in. To not look like a total psychopath, he held only a glimmer of a smile. Unfortunately, the teacher did not feel the same. Steam puffed out of his ears, as his face turned into a red pepper. No one dared to make a peep, all except the crybabies who got hit by the desk.

After a long silence of contemplation, the teacher ground his teeth. "What is your parents' phone number, boy?"

Surprised by his response, the boy refused the teacher's demand, and instead made a flightless bird appear out of thin air.

The puddle faded, and the brass knuckles pulled themselves back to the pedestal. I walked back over to the weapons, taking a deep slow breath. I could feel his dark narcissistic aspirations. There was no order to this place, no landscape anymore, nothing except the dirt under my feet.

It was safe to assume that these weapons were the key to my dark friend's perception of reality. The irony of his world was an insult, to make a mockery of my dream, as if it were nothing more than a gag. I decided to try the old rusty hatchet. As soon as my fingers wrapped around the splintering hickory, I felt a sharp pain shooting through my body, knowing I would have to hurt someone. I turned around and saw five teenagers. They looked at me with an uneasy stare. Three of them charged me. I swung the hatchet randomly. Two of them jumped back, but one was stupid enough to run into the head of the hatchet. His face looked like a squashed mango, and with hatchet getting lodged in his head, one of my other two brave victims tackled me to the ground. The second one grabbed the hatchet out of his friend's neck, aiming to find it a new home in my head. I blinded the man who tackled me to the ground, quickly immobilizing him by breaking his windpipe.

"Please, just walk away. Walk away."

The teen counter-offered with an aim to hack off my arm. Fading back, I pivoted left and shot a right cross into his ribcage. As he tucked in his arms to protect his body, I threw a hook, smashing in his face, and he was out for the count. The hatchet fell to the ground. Picking it up, looking over the rest of the pack, the two of them knew they were fucked. I didn't bother waiting for them to make a move, I just bum-rushed the guy to right. I bashed the hatchet into his skull, swinging several times to make sure the deed was done. Blood splattered all over my face, some on my mouth. Getting leverage through the chest cavity, I pried the hatchet from his skull. Turning around, I saw the last victim was running off into the darkness. I watched as the hatchet soared across the sky. Hearing it whistle through the air, followed by a loud thud as it stuck in his back, I noticed the kid flopped around like a fish. I felt miserable doing

77

this, but I had no choice. I ran over and twisted the hatchet, and heard the sound of his spine cracking. Liquid drained from his mouth.

Peering in through the doorway, I glimpsed an elusive-looking man in his early twenties talking to a guy in a hoodie out back, behind the bar. Rats were nibbling on the trash, squeaking. Mold was growing on the side of the dumpster, with broken bottles scattered everywhere across the ground.

"Hey man." The young man twitched.

"Yeah, whatchu lookin' for? Angel dust, cherry bomb, Dan's favorite?"

"Just whatever, man, come on! I just NEED something." Sounding anxious, he stood picking at his skin on one wrist.

The guy grabbed something from his coat pocket and handed him a little bag of blue pills. The young man handed the guy a wad of cash and took off.

The scenery faded to a small dark apartment. It reeked of cat and dog shit. The oven had exploded. Food had been left out for days and the flies were crawling it. Black and green molds looked to be the dominant inhabitants of the apartment. The only light source that worked was the TV and all that played was some softcore porn. Dirty torn-up clothes were scattered everywhere, from the

78

clawed-up couch to the badly stained toilet, which contained a soaking yellowish-white sock.

A glass table stood in the center of the room, in front of the TV with all sorts of drugs laid out on it. There was a bong made from a soda bottle, several burnt spoons, stained syringes. Dozens of different pills and prescription bottles were scattered, each bearing someone else's name. Several joints on their last puff stained the couch. A man creaked in, crouched on his knees against the table, and started to crush the blue pills with a coffee mug that was leaking fluid onto the floor. Trying to do it properly, he slipped a credit card from his wallet and began to scrape little blue lines – three of them. Reaching into his coat pocket, he found a cut-down plastic straw. His hands were shaking as he edged it up into his nose and snuffed the first line. The man coughed a bit, and he knelt wide-eyed for a few seconds. He deeply exhaled while wagging his face like a dog. Afterward, he tipped back on the couch and lay there quietly, watching the softcore porn on the TV.

5: Carefree Monster

IT HURT TO ROLL MY EYES OPEN when the vibration in my pocket erupted. I dug my hand inside to see who felt enough entitlement to actually bother me. Of course, Phil was calling. Displeased by this disgusting beast, I answered it, but only because I knew he would keep calling.

"Hmmm," I answered in a bearish fashion.

"Dude where are you at? I've sent you several messages on the location, and dude, the hot chicks! Get down here! This will-" I decided to hang up on him.

The phone was now filled with obnoxious texts. Phil waiting in line. Phil in the club, Phil at the bar, even Phil taking a selfie while dancing. Scrolling through a few more of his distasteful texts, I came to a video clip. I ticked play, but all I could hear was the booming pop music – lousy audio with more background noise than music. Phil then smiled into the camera, sticking his tongue out like a dog. The video zoomed out to a wider shot; I assume because he had some other prick hold it for him. A sexy-dressed woman was lying on a row of tables. She wore a very low-cut top with something almost big enough to pass off as a short skirt. With her lack of threading, and the camera angle contributing, you could see that her underwear was a perfect match for the outfit.

Phil poured from a bottle of tequila into her bellybutton, and then he continued to suck on it for an uncomfortable length of time after the tequila had to be gone, then he crowed a "Wahoo" with excitement. The woman grinned and pulled him down. At this point I stopped watching, but I noticed that the video clip went on for another minute and a half.

Life felt too short to be in this office at this very moment. Crazily enough, though, Phil being his dumbass-self convinced me to go down to the club.

Swinging out the front door and looking up at the sky, I saw it was a full moon, but freezing cold, and the dirty air never smelt fresher. Walking down the bleak sidewalk, I saw far too many half-witted insects. They put their hands out for money, begging for my mercy. At one point a child, looking all ragged, got all teary-eyed at me. But I swaggered on down the street.

On the way, I could see more irritants living their daily lives, being reckless, as usual. So I decided to tip the scales and have a little fun. There was a man walking outside a restaurant wearing a nice grey blazer. Headed in my direction was a young woman, looking fairly nice, wearing high heels, and carrying coffee. I kicked a few stones while strolling along. Lucky for me, the woman stumbled onto one, and fell forward. As she made her descent toward the concrete, her arms waved in the air, spilling the black coffee onto the man's expensive blazer. His face was priceless. It looked like a snake trying to unhinge its jaw to catch the staining liquid in its mouth. By the time she kissed the ground, the damage had been done. He started yelping, while the woman cried over her broken nose.

Delightful. Let's cause some more havoc, shall we? There was an old man with a cane walking down the sidewalk. Being quiet, I sneaked up behind him and tapped him on his right shoulder. When he turned to look, I kicked his cane down, with him following after it. A couple was walking toward me, and another man was climbing out of a cab at the curb. As soon as I passed the couple, I gave the woman a nice behind-the-back ass slap. I gave no suggestion for any of these idiots to think it was me. The boyfriend freaked; he grabbed the guy exiting the cab, throwing him up against the cab door.

What to do? What next? There was a liquor store across the street; the smell of puffed cigars and beer burps engorged my nose. The cashier was a fat old lard, his clothing stained, but the interior of the store was the exact opposite. The whole room featured fine oak wood. Glass bottles of whiskey were lined up on glossy black shelves. I couldn't help but ogle them. Wines were lined up in petite cubbies, whispering, begging me to open them. Champagne stuck its head out of the corner trying to get my attention, but I'm not one for bubbles. In the center of the room was a tall pyramid of rum bottles arranged on a small round table. The bottles' labels included a picture of a blindfolded pirate walking the plank.

I grabbed a bottle of whiskey; it was a golden honey brown.

Another customer walked in – a young mother and her two pre-schoolers. She was on her cellphone yelling at whoever was on the other end, "I don't care! My daddy is going to ... No! You can't do that!" and she started to throw a tantrum, as if she were one of her own children stomping around the store.

82

She grabbed a bottle of red wine from a cubby, stomped over to the cashier, snatched a corkscrew from a box on the counter. Popping the cork out, she drained a quarter of the bottle in less than ten seconds.

The cashier didn't say a thing; he just started ringing her up. Being the good Samaritan, I decided to step in and offer assistance. "Hey, do you think that's the best idea with your kids ..."

"Mind your own business, dickhead." She continued to chug the bottle.

Well, if she was going to be a bitch, then I might as well teach her a lesson. I got down on my knees, and motioned the kids over to me. "Hey kids, do you know what the word cunt means?" The kids shook their heads. "Well, it's what your mommy is. Now scram!" I whispered.

The kids scampered back to their mother. "Mommy! Mommy, what's a cunt?"

The mother freaked out and half screamed "Don't say that!" Kids being kids, they started to sing and dance around the store "Cunt! Cunt! Mommy's a cunt!"

"Stop!"

The cashier started to laugh, and the angry woman chased after her children, but like all other children, they had too much energy and were able to stay out of her clutches. While running around the store, one of the children knocked into the round table. The kid fell to the floor, and I could see the table was wobbling. A wave of rum bottles started to sway back and forth. The high point of the pyramid started to collapse on itself and topple down. The mother, now next to me, becoming wide-eyed, showed signs of desperation wanting to save her baby. Across the room the cashier shifted from laughing to grim. Not for the child that could be injured, but for his product that was about to shatter and spill. The first bottle was about to hit the floor, but from what I could see it looked like the kid wouldn't get hurt. That first bottle started a chain, though, and soon after two, three, four bottles followed. I really didn't feel like putting forth any effort toward helping this godawful mother, but I could see the toddler looking into my soul, seeing me, seeking me. Looking back into his eyes, I could see a dreadful life, one which no child should have to bear. I could see that he wasn't afraid to die, nor did he particularly care to live. It was this look that pulled me in. The look that plainly showed he believed his life had no meaning. The far too familiar look that I saw mirrored every night.

There was no time to think, only do. I dove for the child, as shards of broken glass clattered on the floor. Feeling the liquor splash my face, my button-up was soaked with rum and blood. Tiny slivers of glass tore into my skin to find themselves a new home. I was a foot away from the toddler, when I could see a bottle about to crack his skull. My arms stretched as far out as they could. The race to the kid was coming to a close, and it looked to be a hair difference. I pushed the toddler out of the way, and the next bottle smashed to the floor. I covered my eyes hoping I wouldn't be blinded. Rum soaked my eyelashes, my temples, and it took a few blinks and fist rubs to be able to see again. When my vision was mostly restored, I could see the child was okay. The mother immediately swung her baby up in her arms, hugging him for dear life.

The cashier was outraged, yelling at me and the mother. Waving his arms, and pointing his finger at the toddlers, he wailed "My store! Do you know how much this is going to cost! You and your fucking kids destroyed everything! You- You- "

Mom then changed her attitude from a caring parent back to a raging bitch again. "Excuse me! You almost got my son killed! I owe you money? What about the shit show I just witnessed? Because you were too careless to even put bottles on a shelf!"

They argued for another minute or two. My conclusion was to grab a few bottles of whatever I could find and be on my way. Saving someone's life gives you a pass not to pay for alcohol, right? Either way that cashier can go screw himself.

Walking down the street at night is always an adventure. There's no crowded sidewalks, no crazy freaks preaching about some mystic-woowoo babble, no one to bug me. It was all replaced with bright light, the night owls who roam the dark shadows, and the occasional prostitute hoping to make a quick buck. A few of them catcalled at me as I walked by, trying to woo me in and steal the hard-earned cash in my wallet. Being the kind of person who's not looking for an STD, I strolled on.

Finally I got to the club. A huge line crowded along the wall of the building. Lines are for losers, and I refuse to wait in them. My plan of attack was to strut on up to the front of the line and act like the biggest baddest douche.

"Name?" asked the bouncer with biceps the size of my head.

"Lib."

"You're not on the list," he snarled, not looking at his clipboard.

"Oh, check again, it may be under-" raising the whiskey bottle up to his eye level.

The bouncer stared at me, trying to decide what to do; he took the bottle and gave me a little nod to proceed.

Walking down the hallway, I could see a door on the other side with lights flying and people raving, the vibrations from the booming music dancing through my body. As I got closer, I could hear people screaming. Walking in was a red carpet leading me to the dance floor. Another two hulk-like men stood next to the entrance. Moving toward the dance floor, my body heated up and sweat dripped on my neck. People were grinding on each other and exchanging saliva. This was not my kinda place. Pushing through the crowd of animals, I reached the bar. A lady with a well-designed skull tattoo on her shoulder mouthed the words through the deafening music, "What do you want?"

I yelled over the music. "I'm looking for a guy, he's kind of an ass, and acts like a wannabe stud."

"That's every guy in here."

I pulled out my phone and showed her the video. She pointed over to the V.I.P. section. Phil was sitting down with that same girl he sucked juice out of, and a few others as well. Shoving past the drunks and meth-heads, I reached the V.I.P. section.

"Phil! What are you doing?" I tried to step over the rope, but was stopped by another meathead.

"Dude! You made it!" Phil motioned the bouncer to let me in.

Phil handed me a drink, and started babbling on about how "popping" this party was and that it was "on fleek." I took a seat next to the sparkley girls. I tossed the champagne out onto the floor, and refilled the glass from my other bottle of whiskey.

"Wait, so how did you get in here?" I asked, while sipping from my drink, only slightly interested.

"They think I'm this rapper named E-Fame. They gave me bottle service, and then these chicks started hoarding me, asking me to sign their boobs, and do shots off of them. Next thing I know I'm in the V.I.P. lounge with these fine ladies!" Wrapping his hands around them.

"Okay, what about the real E-Fame? Where is he?"

"How should I know? Just go with it dude, and par-tay!"

I sat there watching the flock of animals dance. Their lives lost, with no one to guide them. Drunken girls fell to the floor, passed out from all the alcohol in their system. Strangers would drag them from the dance floor. Shots were swigged and beer bottles hoisted. The hostesses were harassed, verbally and physically. Muscular men, with shirts two sizes too small, ground themselves on women half their size.

"What's your name?" asked the girl next to me, trying to engage me in unwanted conversation.

"John," I said, "and you're the girl E-Fame did a shot off of."

"Oh yeah, he said he would pay me fifty bucks."
She pushed her hair back.

"Has he paid you yet?"

"No."

"Then you aren't going to get your fifty dollars."

"Awesome." She said all of this in a focused monotone.

"How is that awesome?"

"I was kidding."

Scanning the room, I could see people pumping their fists in the air, along with other things. It made me wonder how did everyone get here. Not literally, but what symbolic force landed them here to waste their money on overpriced booze and deafening music. The drugs being passed around on the dance floor I could understand, but they all just seemed so careless – or carefree – or both.

The lady next to me yelled over the music, into my ear, "Do you want to get out of here? I know a much cooler spot, better than this shithole."

Going with the flow, I decided to see where the night would take me. "Lead the way," I told her.

She grabbed my hand, but I broke free from her clutches. She found this a little odd; ignoring my frustrated reaction, she headed into the back of the club, where the music was more thumping vibration than sound. There was a door. Walking in, I could see another hallway, and it looked like a 1960s sex room. The walls and ceiling were a soft red fuzzy carpet, and the floor was squishy/sticky black plastic. When we got to the end, there was a waterfall of beads covering the doorway. Pushing the strung beads aside, I could see a very broken-in bed that matched the hallway.

"What is this?" she asked, trying to sound seductive.

I turned around, and she pushed me back to fall on the bed. She started to crawl over me, and began to undo my belt.

"Stop," I warned her.

"What, baby, you don't like this?" and she started nibbling on my ear.

I tried pushing her away, but she latched onto me. There was no satisfaction in this, she was smiling, wanting more. No pleading or begging. It was distasteful, rude. I pushed her aside onto the bed.

"You're no fun!" she pouted.

"Yeah? I bet you have lots of fun."

She got up from the bed and started running her hands over my chest, "You really are going to say no ... to me."

"Yes, and I mean yes. Listen to the diction. Not yes that means no, or no that means yes. Not in any other way do the words coming out of my mouth mean anything except the dictionary terms that they are defined as." I shriveled back when she ran her hands through my hair.

"Is baby feeling insecure?"

"You really don't want to push me."

"Or what, baby's going to get a little angry?" she whispered in my ear, with her hand sliding down my pants, striking a nerve.

I couldn't help it, I threw her against the wall.

"What's wrong baby? Not hot enough for you yet?"

Tears rolled down her face, terrified of the warrior that now stood in front of her.

"I think you just need a drink. Loosen up, no need to get protective of yourself." I poured some of the whiskey on her head.

She sat there frozen. Both tears and whiskey ran down her face, and I couldn't help but wonder what it would taste like. I ran my tongue from the bottom of her cheek to the center of her forehead. It was interesting. Salty with an old light wooden flavor, and a hint of fruit, along with an after taste of makeup. I grabbed the neck of the bottle and smashed it on the ground to make a stabbing instrument. Placing a slight pressure against the center of her neck, I watched as a small stream of blood started to leak.

My mouth suddenly felt like it hadn't touched a drop of water in weeks, and the relentless spout of fruit juice looked very refreshing. Just a sip? Leaning in, to quench the undying thirst, excitement stirred through me. A millisecond before coming in contact with the sweet red, a tear fell on my cheek. Frustrated by the interruption, I look back up to see her sobbing, waiting for me to finish. The show she put on was overdone. A mess of bodily fluids was mixing around us. The romance was gone; all that was left was an insignificant night.

Releasing the pressure from her neck, I asked, "Where's your purse?"

The "scared for her life" look wasn't going to work.

"Hello, hey, where is your purse?" I asked again.

She quivered out the letters V-I-P.

Snapping my fingers at her, I commanded her to stay.

I walked out and went to the V.I.P. section. Phil was still there, canoodling with the rest of the slim slabs of meat. The rock-for-brains bouncers were kind enough not to hassle me, and one lifted the velvet rope. It took a second, but I was able to find the purse. Strolling on back to the poorly designed bedroom room, I found her ID. She was sitting in the same spot, like a good little girl.

"Look at me, here, look at me. This right here. Do you see that? That is your ID. Which means I know where you live. If you try to contact the police or tell anyone else about tonight, then next time I won't be so nice. Understand?"

She gave me a slight nod.

"Good." I slid the ID into her bra.

Might as well look in her wallet, see if there's anything worth taking. Forty-one dollars.

Walking out of the room, I had no intention of following up on her. If she were to get hold of the cops, there would be no way for me to get to her in time. Even if I did, by the time I would know about it, they would have already arrested me. That dumb bitch probably is too afraid to speak up anyway. A cold breeze hit me in the face walking outside. Looking down at the ground, I remembered all the scratches on my chest; the shirt had soaked up most of the blood. How interesting, I was able to get in the club with a blood-stained shirt, just by bribing the bouncer with booze? It feels unprofessional to be wearing a torn shirt out in public.

The time was now 3:29 a.m. All the shops were closed, and no tailor I know of will work with me at this hour. I made my way back to the office, passing by several hobos warming up next to burning trash cans; the same hookers I'd walked by before attempted to entice me with sex again, along with other nonsense. Finally, a tolerable looking simpleton came along in my direction. His button-up shirt looked like a black underlayer with hundreds of blue circles covering the whole shirt.

"Excuse me, how much for your shirt?"

He looked at me as if I were an idiot like him. "What?"

"Your shirt, I wish to purchase it."

"Sorry, what?"

"I'm sure someone at your caliber of gray matter will be able to savvy my dilemma. So how much for the shirt?"

"Gray matter? Dude, what *are* you talking about? Speak proper English!"

It would be much easier to kill him or at least knock him out, and then leave him in a dumpster half naked, but there are cameras everywhere now, and I don't need to be sued right as I just got back. "Listen very carefully. Take this fifty dollars, put it in your pants pocket, and give me your shirt." I handed him a few bills from my wallet.

As the half-naked man walked away, I undressed myself. The sleeves were a little tight, but there was no point in complaining. A few more minutes and I'd be in my office sound asleep, away from all of these creatures.

6: Man in the Pink Suit

THE ROOM WAS DARK, AND A CROWD of people were sitting in a small space. Looking down, a stage performance, and by the looks of it, Shakespeare's *Macbeth* was the entertainment. The elderly woman next to me smelled like she'd been dipped in a vat of cheap perfume. Sitting next to her was a promise to my sinuses of a long and painful death. Rising out of my seat, purposely stepping on everyone's toes, then walking toward the exit, I got a whiff of the horrid performance. Macbeth made long dramatic pauses, then screamed at random points. People were applauding and cheering. Why God made such a fatuous species is beyond me. No one in this room had a speck of intelligence. Learning the ins and outs of taxidermy would be more interesting than watching this performance.

"Boo!" I shouted.

"To be or not to be. That is the question!" the actor roared.

I walked faster. "Come, come, you wasp," he shouted, "in faith, you are too angry!"

"Wrong play, asshole!" I screamed at him.

Leaving the auditorium, I found myself in the men's restroom. The room was completely empty. To the right were four urinals, each with a little perpendicular wall for privacy. Beyond the urinals were three stalls that had fine white paint. On the other side of the restroom were the sinks. There looked to be automatic soap dispensers, and the faucets were long stainless tubes that came out from the wall, which was just a large mirror. The actual sink itself was a premium white marble stone that looked so clean that a person could spend hours looking for a single water mark and still find nothing. The flooring was black tile, in the shape of bricks. I took a few steps, and stood in front of one of the sinks, glaring at glass reciprocity, seeing the hateful man standing in front of me. The man that wanted to end it all, and leave everything behind. The thing in the reflection let out a booming roar, screaming at me to be released. The floor beneath my feet shook. Then silence. Hundreds of tiny spiders seemed to crawl beneath my skin, webbing a fake smile for me as a disguise. I scrunched my cheeks and forehead, trying to make the tingling stop. It didn't work. I scratched, picked at the dead skin, clawing at the jaw.

A flask filled with whiskey was in my inner coat pocket. Twisting the lid off, and putting the mouth of the flask to my nose, I inhaled and smiled; the aroma was divine, but God deserved less. It reminded me of a placid day of relaxation, no social interaction, just quiet.

"Here's to you, the dumb fuck that brings me immortality. And to me, the only one who truly understands you in this psychotic fucked-up world."

95

Taking in some relief, my mind started to feel more at ease, but was soon after interrupted by a man slamming the far left bathroom stall open. He was fat, bald, possibility in his late thirties or early forties. He had a nickel-sized mole under his right eyebrow that made it distracting to try to focus on the rest of him. His beard flowed all directions, making him look raggedy. The clothing he wore was substantial, a bright pink suit – yes, pink – with a white waistcoat and button-down shirt and a gray tie. This devilish looking madman stood there, eyeing me like a piece of meat.

It wasn't until I said something, he decided to leave. The door slam echoed. Finally alone, I took a mammoth-sized whiskey gulp. The feeling of loneliness was mind-numbingly calm, and yet it was upsetting. No need to make small talk or discuss opinions on the weather. Silence was more of a blessing than winning the lottery.

When I turned to leave the bathroom, though, there stood a bathroom attendant. He stood stiff with a bland bored look, but his eyes told a different tale. They spoke to me saying, "Wow, this guy is pretty weird, and why is he talking to himself? Hey that guy in the pink suit was looking pretty slick. Why am I even here? My job is pointless. I could literally be replaced by a hand dryer or a paper towel dispenser." *Okay, he's looking at me weird. Maybe we are in a staring contest. Ah shit! He's going down!*

I slowly stepped forward and looked him dead in the eye. The towel resting on his arm was very soft and fluffy. Not my preferred type – rugged and crusty, with no fabric softener, takes in the water much easier. Grabbing the towel resting on his arm, the saliva on the back of my tongue was making it harder to breathe. Tossing the towel aside, I grabbed my wallet. There were several twenties, one five, and five ones. I grabbed the five ones and held it out in front of the attendant. He extended his other arm with an open palm. The five ones fell into his hand. Now facing the exit door, I saw a picture on the door of a young man who looked to be from the 14th century, holding a skull, looking very dramatic. It hung there on the door and beneath it was lettered "to pee or not to pee," by far the worst bathroom humor I've ever encountered.

The bathroom attendant, still standing like a statue, stared at me, waiting for me to leave. To even be within a mile of this garbage was terrible enough, and here this man sits by as hundreds, maybe thousands, of people come into these chambers and see this insult of comedy. Retribution must be served.

The only way to do it was by his relinquishing one of the dollars I'd just gifted to him, which he had not actually rightfully earned. When I tried retrieving my dollar bill, though, the attendant was hesitant. He clenched his fist and tried to hide dollars behind his back. It took me a minute, but he learned not to leave his hand out, a perfect opportunity for biting. Walking out of the bathroom, I felt satisfied with how that had played out.

In the short time I'd been gone, it seemed the audience had doubled in size, and to make matters worse, it felt even more crowded and compacted than it really was.

This time, there was no choice but to step on everyone's toes. While I made my way back toward my seat, a few of the audience members were kind enough to relinquish their snacks. They tried to stop me, but as I noted earlier, it was impossible.

Collapsing back in my chair, my shoulders felt like they were touching the nipples of the people to the left and right of me. With my arms thereby in bear-trap restriction, my ability to munch on my recently acquired snacks was constrained. These were little colorful balls. Tossing one at a time in the air and catching it in my mouth, I thought they tasted sweet, filled with chocolate and peanuts. Almost immediately, though, the chocolate melted, which left the nut by its lonesome.

I can never tell if my chewing is too loud. Not that other people's opinions matter, they don't, it's just my curiosity. The chewing did seem loud to me. It sounded like plastic grinding on cement. The box of chocolate fell to the floor. I went to pick it up and there was this strange feeling that someone was watching me from afar. Looking to my right I saw the man from the bathroom stall was over there in the aisle, staring at me.

"The hell?" I whispered.

The older lady on my right shushed me.

This is easily one of the rudest things a person can do to set me off. Oh, how I would love to smash her head in, my knuckles soaking in blood, making her face look like a bundt cake. Her left eye would be forced into her shattered skull, while the right popped out of its socket. I'd pierce her neck to make her *my very own puppet.*

"How about that airplane food, eh?" she would say, and give a huge unhinging jaw laugh.

We could wow the crowd with my ventriloquism. People would praise me.

"Encore! Encore!" they'd cheer.

I could almost feel the beaming incandescent light focused on me, sweat rolling down my face, all eyes on me. That is what people truly want to see. *That's real entertainment.*

But if I were to lay one finger on her, some pig head would hold me down – I just knew it. Like every other dream and prayer, this one will never come true.

Flipping back to reality, I saw now the restroom man was out of sight, probably just returned to the lobby. I squeezed back up into my chair, so ready for this nightmare to be over. Five seconds went by, and it felt like a year. I can't leave; this had already cost far too many crab legs. Let's be honest, at least the play is better than having a conversation with others.

A murmur came from behind me. I tried to ignore it, but it just kept on. The murmurs went from a soft conversation to an outside-voice discussion. They were talking about how *Macbeth* doesn't make any sense. Which was false; the play's pretty straightforward. All this chatter was badly distracting me from the play. Do adults really seriously honestly need to be told to shut the fuck up in a theatre?

Turning around and glaring at them, I hissed, "Hey can you please be quiet. Some of us actually want to watch this." I sounded like a prick, but I had good reason.

The old lady on my right shushed me again.

"Sorry, what's the problem?" the young man behind me said, holding what looked to be his girlfriend's hand.

"You're interrupting the play. Can you please be quiet?"

They gave me a haughty "Fuck off" look and returned to their conversation.

"Seriously!" I nimbly threw a chocolate candy at the girlfriend's head.

"Listen pal, why don't you-" the boyfriend said aggressively, just before I cut him off.

"No! *You* two need to shut the fuck up, and respect the-" again I was shushed by the old lady. I turned to her and growled quietly, "I swear, if you shush me one more time, I will slit your throat and swim in your blood!" I noticed I was grinding my teeth.

She gave me a severe and scolding look and returned to minding her own business.

"Listen, we're just trying to have a good time here, so why don't you go back to watching and we won't have a problem," he said. His girlfriend wrapped herself around him.

I swear was going to break a blood vessel. Taking a deep breath in, I softly said, "If you don't shut up now, I'm going to cut off your fingers and feed them to your girlfriend."

"Dude, she's my sister!"

"Why are you fucking your sister?"

"I didn't say I- oh never mind, jeeeesus, mind your own business, pal!"

"As soon as-" I heard a call some coming from behind me, ahead of us. Turning back around, now facing the stage again, I saw the actor playing Macbeth was looking at and directly speaking to me. I stood up, and he went on.

"Hey sir, if you don't be quiet, you will have to leave."

"But they're the one-"

"Sir! Sir, please take your seat, so everyone can enjoy the show," Macbeth said.

It was pointless to argue, so I sat back down and returned to watching the play. I could feel the smirks on the incest couple's faces behind me. Being that they were delinquents, it was only fair to assume they were giving me the bird, and then some, behind my back, so I showed the same courtesy.

Why can't this play just end already?

A deep yawn crept up my throat, and I started to get teary-eyed. Not wanting to look weak, I wiped the eye droplets away. Something hit the right side of my face. There was a little trickle on me and whatever it was hit the floor. I looked down to see what it was, but the floor was just a black hole. Probably just my imagination. A few seconds later, something definitely hit me. Looking to the right I saw the man in the pink suit, throwing little hard candies at me. That shitbird. He made a smug grin in my direction, and even though he sat several seats away, it was obvious he needed dental work. Gawd, what fucking next?

I'd had it with this place, with these people, and with this play. I got up from my seat, and I walked quickly over to confront the problem. He could tell I was pissed as he saw me coming, and he jumped out of his seat and ran off, up the aisle to the double doors. Hauling ass, I chased after him. He had a head start and was ahead of me when we reached the lobby. Sprinting through the doors, I found myself in the concession area. Where was that bastard?

"Hey!" I confronted the bartender. "Did you see a man in a pink suit come through here? He has a mole on his face that's large enough to be seen from space!"

"We get a lot of people like that in here. What's his name?"

No help, not from that idiot. I continued the hunt. Beyond the bartender's station, the lounge was softly lit and nearly empty.

Being ever so quiet, I tiptoed into the lounge area. Pressing my back against the wall, I peeked around the corner. Nothing. The lounge itself was quite pleasing to the eye. Fine dark wood throughout, mahogany maybe, with polished brass and etched glass. The huge stone fireplace burned white flames with green highlights – a nice touch. I wondered now why I'd never come in here before. Too late now.

Over to the right and down the wall a ways was the men's room. The door opened with a squeeeeek as I pushed through, but it was nearly empty, just a leaky sink faucet echoing in the tiled room.

My attention turned to the bathroom attendant. Weirdly enough, it was the same guy. Giving him a glare, and a little head nod of acknowledgement, I saw he stuck his hand out for another tip. Fair is fair, I guess. Digging through my front pocket I found lint and a game token. It was priceless, because it said "no cash value."

The man bowed backward out the door, so I prowled over to the first stall and kicked it open. Nothing. Next stall over. Kick and a slam. Nothing. Next one. Nothing. At the last stall door, I kicked it hard enough that I made a literal hole through the painted particle board, snagging my shoe. The stall, though, also was empty, like the rest.

I freed my foot from the door and backed up. Getting up close to the mirror, seeing all the minor details, I made useless facial expressions: scowling, screaming, crying.

"You piece of shit. Why? Why are you like this? Why?" I yelled. I slammed my head against my face in the glass.

There was a knock at the door.

"Occupied!"

The door opened.

"I said *occupied*!"

The bathroom attendant walked back in, along with a man wearing a yellow blazer. Most likely the manager. I spat in the sink and gagged, pretending to be sick.

"Is everything all right in here, sir?"

Making a gag noise, I wretched out "No" and spat into the sink again.

"Can we get you anything, sir?" the manager asked.

"Coke and whiskey, on the rocks."

The attendant stayed, peering at me, and the manager left – either to grab the drink or call the cops.

The manager returned, actually carrying a drink, but instead of my coke and whiskey, it was a long twist of orange peel floating in a clear liquid in a stem glass. I snatched it from him, swigged the drink down. He and the attendant guy stared at me.

As I walk back through the bar and into the auditorium, it seemed the room was shaking from all the excitement. People were cheering and being overdramatic. I made my way back to my seat, stepping on everyone's toes yet again. When I got near, I saw the little shit in the pink suit had stolen my spot.

"Um ... that's my seat."

He turned to look at me. "Sorry, what?"

"You are sitting in my seat," I hissed.

"I believe you are mistaken."

"No! Now get out!"

The old lady shushed me.

Just one swipe of the knife in my pocket. A clean cut from ear to ear.

"Get the fuck out of my seat."

"No!"

"If you don't get out of my seat, I will skin you from head to toe. And use it as a kite for children to play with."

"No." he said, sounding agitated and childish.

Just as I leaned in to strangle him, someone pulled me back, "Hey! Hey! Hey! Is there a problem here?" A uniformed security guard barked from the aisle.

"He is in my seat!"

"No, he is lying," said the shit in pink. "I've been here the entire time!"

The old lady interjected. "This lovely young man has been nothing but a pleasant surprise," she started. "Then this ugly fellow here shows up out of nowhere and starts a ruckus." The couple behind her chimed in to agree with the nasty old bat. Macbeth even felt the need to give his opinion. "It's true!" he called from the stage.

"Sir, why don't you come with me?" the guard said, moving in and laying his hand on my shoulder.

"Don't!"

But I went along with him. As we made our way to the exit, I could hear Macbeth applauding. "Thank you!"

I turned around and shouted, "Go fuck yourself!" After that, the security guy became much more physical.

It was dark outside. The smell of wood smoke on the air was pleasant. Cool enough to put a chill on my face. It was late, peaceful. I found my way back to the apartment building. Floor 38 and room 25, I kicked the door open and found the room was dark, but the hallway brought in enough light to see and to walk around. One of the cupboards must have booze.

Jackpot. The one over the oven held whiskey, rum, and a large bottle of an oak-shaded liquid. I pulled the cork, held it near my mouth ... it smelled of cinnamon. A sip. Another. It went down like soda. Whatever it was, though, it had more of a kick then a can of coke. I chugged some more and enjoyed the spread of warmth from my throat out across my chest.

I found a glass on the counter and poured myself a big one. I sipped my drink this time, actually savoring the moment and the cinnamon taste. Life didn't seem too despicable at this very moment. No one to bother me, no one to tap me on the shoulder and ask me stupid questions, no one to irritate me into strangling them. The emptiness, however, was still there hugging me, strangling me. Inescapable.

Then I noticed the creaking coming from around the corner and across the room. I looked, but all that I could make out out in the dark was a door at the end of the short wide hallway. The creaking continued. A shivering chill ran up my spine. A knife set in a wooden block was set out on the kitchen counter. I grabbed the narrow filleting knife. The blade was five or six inches long, with the dark wood handle adding another six. I moved silently toward the door, and the creaking became louder. Then the door slowly swung open. My body was blocking the light coming from the still-open door to the hallway. I inched forward. Silence. The only thing I could hear was my own breathing and my heartbeat in my ears. I was wound tight, ready to stab whatever was coming to kill me. Nothing. What the serious fuck?

I grabbed the creaky door and swung it shut. The breeze behind the door brushed past me – must be an open window in there. There was a muffled thud, but it wasn't the door. It sounded like it came from the floor. I got on my knees and felt around the side of the door to find out what was blocking it. A shoe. A large man's athletic shoe. Tossing it aside, I got to my feet and pulled the door shut once more. A hand grabbed my shoulder and without any hesitation I spun around and buried the knife in the cold air.

The hallway lights flicked on and nearly blinded me. I looked around quickly from left to right and back, noting there was a couch facing a TV on a low table. I planted myself on the couch, grabbed the remote next to me, and clicked the power on. Some silly sitcom spread across the screen, the volume soft, and one of the characters was telling his friends how he'd just "hooked up with a chick."

There was a knock from the doorway, on the frame of the still-open door. The knife flew from my hand, aimed to kill the intruder. Sadly, the knife hit the doorframe. The guy standing there jumped, startled, and hit the opposite wall in the hallway. He took off running, leaving behind a package. I didn't bother trying to call him back.

I fetched the package and set it on the kitchen counter. I fetched the filet knife from the doorway too, and closed the door. I slit through the packaging, and a box of Double Stuff Oreos sat slid out. I wasn't hungry at the moment, so I turned the lights back out and resettled myself on the couch, then resumed with the TV programming. By the next commercial break my nerves had finally settled. Soon enough the landlord will call, I thought, or the cops, but neither were at the top of my priority list.

My body became one with the couch, and I decided that was how it was going to be for the next eight or so hours. Letting my mind wander off, the darkness became like a cool blanket, cuddling me like a baby. My body slowly sank into the abyss, wishing I could stay there, quiet, alone, forever.

Breathing became a main focus, having to take a deep breath in and then slowly exhale. It was like holding your breath underwater, slowly letting out air a bubble at a time to stay focused.

After a while my eyes sprang open, feeling a tight cord wrapped around my neck. Suddenly gasping for air, attempting to pull loose the cord, I could feel it squeezing the life out of me. I grabbed for whatever was behind me. The attacker pulled me up and over the back of the couch, then down, dragging me by the neck. About to pass out, my vision was fading black. He dropped me, and let go of the rope.

Heaving in great gulps of oxygen, I felt blood leaking from my mouth. Forcing myself up to my feet, a sharp pain rattled my rib cage, and then came a blow to the head, launching me back against the couch. Barely able to focus, I watched a pink blur charge at me, smashing us both across the room and out the window. Out. Out the window from the 38th floor. Jeeeeeeesus.

He latched onto me, screaming, as we fell to our death. A smile unraveled slowly across my face.

Is this really how I die?

7: The Walk of Pain

WAKING UP IN A HOSPITAL BED is never fun, although a breezy backside can be a bit disorienting. A nurse walked in, gave me a dull "*oh, you're awake*" look. Not saying a word, she walked back out. Attempting to sit up, I noted my body ached. I've been in worse condition before, no reason to complain. Now on my feet, I could feel the three broken ribs stabbing me.

"You shouldn't be doing that," an elderly man said from the bed next to me.

"Mind your own business."

The old guy muttered to himself and started fooling with his hospital bed remote.

The IV pole was a little help for stability, and I held tight while searching the room for my clothes.

"Excuse me," a female voice said from behind me. I turned around to see the doctor. "If you could take a seat."

"I prefer to stand."

She took a deep breath, and put on a fake smile, "Okay, can you at least tell me your name?"

"Shouldn't you already know that?"

"Yes, I'm just making sure you know."

I've been awake for less than five minutes and I'm already hating the people around me. "It's lib-liberation."

The doctor looked hesitant, probably assuming I was just an average moron like she has to deal with on a daily basis. She grabbed my clipboard from the front of the bed. "Your x-rays say you have several

112

cracked ribs" – nothing I didn't already know – "and a hairline parietal skull fracture. You may have some memory loss. We induced you into a medical coma to reduce the swelling. You also seem to-"

"Wai, wai, wait! You induced me into a coma. How long have I been out?"

"Sir, if you could please return to your bed."

"How long I have been out!" trying hard to level my temper.

"A week."

I took a deep breath, and tried exhaling all paranoia, tried being the key word. "Where are my clothes?"

"If you can just take a seat-"

"Where are my clothes!" anger slipping through.

"In the drawers under the TV-" before she finished her sentence, I unrobed myself and began to change – "but I highly recommend you stay for observation."

"Listen, I know you're just doing your job, but I'm fine."

"I told him to sit down," the old man added helpfully.

I glared at him. "I'd say drop dead, but it looks like you've been trying for years."

"Fuck you!" the old man waved his finger at me.

"You'd like that, wouldn't you?"

The doctor walked up to me as I put on my pants, and placed her hand on my shoulder. I jumped back, feeling a stabbing pain. "Don't!"

"You have sustained injuries that could cause major brain damage, we need to keep you here for monitoring, you need our help."

"I need? What I need is to leave! Now I have not hurt you or harassed you or anyone else since I've been here."

"What about me, asshole?" the old man said.

"I will rip your fucking tongue out!" I took a half a second, gathered my thoughts, and realized what I had just said. "I apologize. Now, I am going to leave, and you cannot stop me."

The doctor followed me out and down the hall to the nurses' station to find release forms. "I'm placing an order with the hospital pharmacy for some pain medication. You should stay off your feet, and don't drive anywhere."

"Yeah, sure, whatever," half listening to her, I filled out the paperwork. I started to walk off, but stopped myself and turned around. "Where am I?"

"In a hospital, third floor. Elevator is down the hall, take a right, and it should be on your left," she said, sounding like a smartass.

The elevator door slid open, the car was empty. I got in and the door closed, classical music playing in the background – or was it in my head? Either way, the moment was drowning in equanimity. I pushed the first-floor button, leaned back, and closed my eyes. I'm falling, escaping everyone, and everything around me, not having to deal with society. My whole life has just been one big regret. People, so heinous.

Greed is what drives mankind. They may say, "You don't owe me anything." Lies. All lies. For every cause, there is an effect. Kindness is a stab wound that can't heal. It attracts viruses, and bacteria, and causes an infection that can only lead to remorse for what man calls friends and family. Why let pain in? Why go through the suffering just to come out empty-handed? I'd rather bathe in my own blood.

There are over four thousand religions, each with a set of rules more absurd than the last. Thou shall not take what is not given. Consumption of alcohol is a sin. Envy is bad. All these rules, and for what, to praise a higher power? Allah, God, Goddesses, it's all the same. God is good? No pure-hearted being would make humanity the way it is.

We are all just puppets, being played and made to dance by the societies ruling at the time. "I had strings, but now I'm free." Bullshit at its finest.

Our strings are cut when we die. Then, and only then, are we free. Fuck people and religion. Fuck God. Fuck society. Fuck strings.

The elevator made a ding, and the music stopped. The doors opened, and my eyes unrolled. Another well-suited man entered. Looking up, I could see we were at the lobby.

"Fifth floor," he said, looking at me as if I were an elevator attendant.

In return, I gave him a conceited look. "Asshole." I walked out and the doors closed behind me.

It was a quick trip across the lobby past reception and OUT. Exiting the front doors of the hospital, inhaling the air felt like swallowing icicles, the smell still the same – like piss, with a hint of regret. The sky was bleak and nearly colorless. The ground ruined my shoes, covering them with grit and muck. No reason to complain, I guess, what's done is done.

The street was busy, fast traffic, but not terribly crowded. I began the journey by trying to catch a cab. They all sped past me, as if I were invisible. Come on. Not a single one of you insignificant hustlers can stop?

Frustrated with waiting, I stepped out in front of a cab, half hoping it would hit me. There was a loud screech, tire marks blackened the road. It came to a halt inches before it hit me. The cabbie threw his hands up, and started yelling. I walked around to get in the back of the cab.

"Get out!" he yelled.

I handed the driver two twenties. "Here's your tip. Now drive."

The cabbie kept quiet, and followed my commands. Dance puppet, dance. I told him where I lived.

The cabbie looked at me in his rearview. He drove.

A few minutes went by. Everything felt compacted somehow, the people arguing outside, the undying honking between the cars, this cabbie's awful taste in music.

I stared at the back of the cabbie's head. "Look at the worthless piece of shit. He should be dead. He's basically a dog. Please sir, can I have some more money? What a joke," It said. "How easy would it be to just kill him, snap that fat neck of his?"

The cab came to a halt. My apartment was still a few blocks up, but it felt like too much work to get him to keep driving, so I got out and resumed my journey on foot. The driver honked his horn. "You still need to pay me!" he shouted after me.

"The tip should cover it."

He didn't bother arguing, and just drove off.

The dirt scuffing my shoes started to bother me. A few hops in the air, clicking my shoes as I went, helped a lot. I shed enough dirt like that to where it was tolerable. I would have waited, but I had thought I would be home soon enough to clean them off. Stains are not an option; stains are the silent killer. Which reminds me, when did I buy this shirt, it looks new, and the price tag is still on the left pocket button?

Walking into the wind, I had the sound banging inside my head. I rooted in my coat pocket and found a pair of fair-looking earbuds. No point in wasting brain power on people I don't care for.

One thing that does intrigue me is a person's rhythm, the way they walk. Tac- tuc- tooc- tac. Tac- tuc- tooc- tac. Each step takes more and more of your focus. Staring down at their feet, not looking up to see what's ahead – ever watched people walk like that? I was seeing every detail on my shoes, even the little blue speck on the aglet. One bit of stitching is loose, but just to the point where you could slide a .60 mm needle through the loop. It's one of those things, it just itches me the wrong way.

Something brushed my eye.

Looking up, I found myself standing in the middle of a winter forest, moonlight lighting a path. It was cold, but the frost didn't bother me. The pain was actually a nice reminder. My music was gone, and the only sound to be heard now was cold cut snowflakes wisping in the air. My socks took the snow, causing my toes to freeze. But I felt fine. Not a bother in the world. A stream ran down my cheeks quickly freezing over. The coat was no help, and taking it off made me feel warmer. I guess fine isn't the right word, but then neither is the word happy, or even sad. Jaded. Like an unneeded weight. I tilt my head down, open my mouth, and let everything go. I could feel an explosion at the back of my head. Red flowed down my face, dripping from my eyes and nose onto my shirt. The familiar metallic taste staining my mind, forever unclean. The feeling of mortality, a true sensitizer. A glimmer of joy ran dry, and a pool of blood built up beneath my feet, revealing my reflection.

"No! No, no, no, no, no, no!"

The dark shadow stood about thirty feet from me.

"Why are you doing this to me? Do you know what you've put me through? The pain I've had to endure? Knowing that all I had, or ever will have, is taken from me. Do you!"

The thing just stared at me, not having the courtesy to respond.

"ANSWER ME!"

The dark shadow slowly advanced. I sprinted toward the darkness, each step quaking the forest. Ten feet, dark shadow eyes stared into my soul. Five feet, his teeth formed a smile. At two feet, the warm breath burned to the touch. I extend my arms, to bring it to the ground, reaching for its throat, burying my finger under his vocal cords, but my fingers slip through him, as did the rest of my body.

Blind now, and covered in darkness, I ran to find him. Flinging around in a random sequence, I hit my head on something and fell to the ground, only to find myself sitting on my ass, next to a light post. The people paid no attention.

I got up, and continued on. Marching along the sidewalk, the insignificants twiddle their thumbs and puff on their smokes. The sooner I'm home, the better.

A group of hipsters at a corner locked eyes with me, one attempting to hand me a flyer of some sort. Doing the politest thing possible, I pretended I couldn't hear them over the music. The nuisance guy followed me to the end of the block, and then he pulled on my coat. Break his jaw or take the flyer? Break his jaw or take the flyer?

I took the flier, and the hipster ran off. The paper was lathered in a sticky substance, and as I ripped it off my hand, the adhesive was stringy. I crumpled it up, and left it with the rest of the garbage alongside the curb.

There was an old man with a curly beard wearing an eyepatch and playing pots and pans like a lazy drummer, whacking them with a metal spatula and a half-eaten celery stick. The bum had no musical talent. Zero. I would prefer to stand in the engine room of a train, shoveling coal. This pathetic puke was an embarrassment to music. He should be strung up by the toes and beaten to death. I am appalled to know that I exist in a world where a man can be allowed to perform such shit. If I didn't have a microscopic amount of self-respect, I would stab my ears with a rusty pair of scissors. I turned my earbuds up.

There is often a moment in a person's life where they learn to control their emotions. To walk away from the controversy. So far, I've been able to walk away, but if one more person pisses me off, someone's going to be thrown in front of a bus.

A young couple is arguing at a bus stop. My music was too loud to hear the conversation, but the girl was flailing her arms in every direction. She slapped the guy in the face. The boyfriend did nothing. She did it again. He calmly tried to stop her. She became a rollercoaster. There were punches and scratches and windmilling. After a little bloodshed, he caved and locked her in his arms. She started kicking and jumping; I'm not much of a lip reader, but the word "Help" was quite apparent. I looked down at my phone and pretended like nothing was happening, and really nothing was happening. I looked up to see the girl headbutt her boyfriend. Then, unfortunately, she broke free and latched onto me. My cracked ribs howled. I tried shaking her off; when that didn't work, I ran her into a brick wall. My plan was unsuccessful, but it did knock out my ear buds and knock her off my arm. This bitch was causing me more pain than the busted ribs.

"GET OFF!"

The boyfriend then stepped in.

"Babe! Come on! Babe! Babe!"

I ran her into the bus stop shelter, hitting her head on a metal bar, and she was out like a light. For a moment I could see the indentation from where she hit her head, fascinating.

The boyfriend freaked out and charged at me.

I pivoted and threw a hook straight into his face. He toppled over and fell onto the sidewalk, out cold too.

"Nope, nope, nope." I walked away from the shit show.

Music's good while running, it lets the mind feel at ease. At least there was one upside to all of this. Made my mark on this town, I did, and there were no cameras around to record my fleeing from the scene. Win-Win.

At my apartment building, though, the elevator said, "out of order." Just my luck. Thirty-eight floors, here we come. My head felt like it had been hit by a jackhammer. Is napping on the stairs an option? Is it worth having some stranger dipping in my pockets while I'm passed out from exhaustion? It's a close call, but sleep on my own floor does beat being stabbed. The first step is always the hardest? False. Whoever said that should be executed.

By the fifth floor my legs had the consistency of a worm. People were smoking cigarettes in the stairwell, and drinking bourbon beyond the open doors in the hallways. I didn't personally smoke, but the smell wasn't displeasing to me. Trying to act cool, I walked up to a couple of them, and gave them tired smile.

"Hey?" a guy said, somehow making it sound like a question.

A few awkward moments went by before actual words came out of my mouth. "The ah ... the bottle. You mind?"

The guy leaning against the door stepped back into his apartment and a few seconds later reappeared with a pink coffee cup. His friend had a heavy hand when pouring me some.

"Thanks," I bowed gratefully in his direction and drained the cup.

Back to my seemingly endless journey. By the seventh or eighth floor, I was butt scooting up the stairs, giving my screaming leg muscles a change. At one point some drunken clown was butt-scooting past me down the stairs, and we got to talking.

This old bozo was laying some deep philosophical knowledge out on the table. He had wild white hair and mismatched clothes and had on clown socks. He said his name was David. "Think about it, our lives are just a blink in time. And all we do is worry about what our hair looks like, and if our shoes match our shirts. People need to get over themselves, man. It like.. What's the point. You and I ... we see eye-to-eye to eye ... to eye. Hehehehe." It began to dawn on me the guy wasn't drunk, just nuts. "Four eyes," he said, "four eyes. I think the best thing for us to do is just live our lives the best we can do. Men and women are so different, you see, it's all hormones. Look at me! I just fucked up with the birthday boy's mom, and I'm happy as a clown. The world is an imperfect place! Hahahahaha!"

"Yeah, but don't you ever get bored with life?" I asked him. "You know. The same thing over and over. I feel tired, you know. Like what's the point? People are so critical. *Oh, he's off standing on top of a building to get attention.* Like, I'm not looking for that. I'm just here for as long as my deal stands. Then when it's over, I'm gone."

I snickered as I told him, "That feeling, always there, reminding me of how boring and humiliating life is. Imagining all the ways to escape, and yet, here I am, still standing!"

The clown soberly said, "Actually you're sitting."

"I feel a constant pain of nothingness," I told him. "Not being able to make connections with anyone. Ever. No one's like me. I'm not like them. I feel this bleak darkness inside that I know won't ever cease until I die. Seeing everything and everyone in a dark perspective, in the sole purpose, just to not feel regret in finding falsified hope."

The clown chuckled. "Your breath is warm."

I got up onto my feet and did a little stretch. "Dance with me," I said, lending a hand to help him to his feet. We grabbed each other's waists, and slowly danced up and down the stairwell. We nearly toppled down the stairs and broke our necks, but that made it all the better. Back and forth, careful not to step on each other's toes, resting our heads on each other's shoulders. At one point Mr. David got a little handsy with me, but that didn't kill the moment. Him pitching a tent is what killed it.

Pulling away, I told him, "I hope our paths cross again someday."

The clown leaned in for a kiss, but I stopped him by laying my finger on his lips.

"Let's not ruin the moment." Then I pushed him down the stairs, where he could nap on the landing. "Good night, good night! Goodnight till it be morrow," and then up I continued on my own journey to find my own sweet slumber. The handrail was helpful, until it disappeared after the floor nineteen wall.

"You never slow danced with me like that." It sounded jealous.

"You think about putting people's heads on chopping blocks."

"I don't see the correlation."

"meh"

"Bozo David the clown was right, you know. Living free, it's what sheds out the weak."

"It's a good thing I'm still standing."

"You have all this potential, and you waste it on mindless efforts to blend in. Think of-"

"Enough with the lectures already. I know who I am, and I know what I want. You can't change me. What makes you think I can be changed? I'm not a piece of play-doh that can be molded into whatever you want. Put me in a cage, and I will find a way out. Give me a knife, and there will be a feast. Hand me a pen, and I'll burn you so deeply that you might as well give up now, because you're worthless garbage ... the little dust particles a ninety-year-old grandma sweeps away, when cleaning her sad little nursing home room. Fucking grit under fingernails that's scraped and disposed of. A voice whispering in my ear, driving me insane. Making everyone around me think I'm crazy. You call society the monster, then what are you, the savior? Some higher power to guide civilization into a new era of eternal peace? Guess what, peace is the lie that people use to find fair ground. A temporary standoff amongst the people, to flatter one another. Making a mask called normal. It's a load of shit some entrepreneur used as a sales pitch. It's a word that society uses to find common ground, constantly changing, being manipulated so that everyone is on their toes. I spit on it, because normal is society's monster, but you

... you are mine. You are forever the monster in my closet."

There was a long pause.

"You can call me a monster, but there is one clear difference between me and the people out there. I never lied to you, and that is not something anyone else can say. I am the only one you can trust, and when everyone else has left, I'll be there, because that's who I am and how I do it. The monster in your closet, the one that protects you from the monsters wearing masks that tuck you to bed. The monster that sees the manipulation in the world. The monster that sees you for you."

I didn't bother responding. Nothing to say.

Finally, the twenty-fifth floor. Pushing myself through the door into my apartment, I thought a floor never felt so good. I swallowed the top of my vomit three times, as I staggered my way to the bathroom. Removing the shirt off my back, I saw bandages covering my stomach. Peeling off the tape and cotton, I saw they looked like slashes, but not from an animal's claws. The cuts were wide, both short and long, some deep and gnarly, others nearly faded. My hands lightly brushed over them. Running my fingers down the lining of the cuts. Trying to remember what caused these. It was impossible to tell whether it was the booze, or whatever the hospital had given me, but I was now numb from head to toe. Blood slowly leaked out of the biggest wound. It felt like a warm waterfall trickling down my leg, filling the crevices of the tiled floor next to my foot.

I decided I would put the bandages back on. Rummaging through drawers, I found a roll of plastic wrap, and started wrapping it around my abdomen. I took my pants off, and got in the shower. The blood washed away down the drain. The plastic wrap sagged. Water ran down my face.

After drying myself off, and taking a seat on the couch, I tipped over and passed out buck naked.

8: Finding the Fear

ALLING THROUGH THE DARK ABYSS, a mix of feelings slid to the surface. At one point, plummeting to my death felt quite relaxing, but to know this was all a dream made it into a discomfort. The wind rushed through me, as my heart pounded, adrenaline pumping through my veins. Oh, how I envy that feeling, jealous of the appearance it takes on. Didn't matter the situation, he always felt comfortable with it all. The desire for no ambiguity crawling under my skin. It's unfair, but that's life, and here I am skydiving in this bleak hollowness.

I hit the dirt and turned my back into a gummy worm.

Getting to my feet, I touched my toes, popped my back. Little to say, except that it was not a pleasing experience.

Awesome, back in his memoir. Let's recap: Dirt-cold ground? Check. Bleak sky with no stars or sparkling lights? Overwhelming sense of despair? Check. The pedestals to choose my next victim? Hurray! Dead bodies? Check.

I walked over to the pedestals, and looked at the choices. Rope, gardening tools, a shield. There was a wooden-handled knife with the blade's tip curving inward, kind of like a hawk's beak. There it stood. And an old man standing, with the help of a cane.

To kill out of defense can feel justifiable, smashing those boys' brains in with the hatchet is fair to say not erroneous. This man that stood in front of me, he was weak. His wobble, even with the help of the cane, was quite apparent. There was a look in his eyes that prompted pity. I kicked him to the ground, and covered his face. It was hard to look. The knife tore through the skin like a well-cooked salmon. My hands were swimming in blood and guts, feeling all types of squishy toys. He cried and screamed as I worked my way up. The old man struggled, but I laid a knee on him to find stability. The knife got hooked on something large, I believed it to be the sternum. Yanking and pulling, the man ceased to struggle. Peeking my eyes open, I saw the damage that had been done. It was appalling to see the monstrosity. Sliding my hands off his face, tears mixed in with the dirt.

The liquid drained from his nose and mouth. Pushing the corpse aside, I peered into the memory. It was a younger me, maybe mid-twenties. He was sitting in the car. The radio was softly playing. He held a prescription bottle with the name "Liberation" on it, and the word Fluphenazine below it. The boy brought the bottle to his ear, and slowly shook it. He brought it back in front of his face, seemingly fixated on it.

Shoving the bottle in his coat pocket, he adjusted the rearview mirror, so he could see his eyes. I watched as I let out an echoing wail, not out of rage or passion, but in hopes of feeling something. He got out of the car, and walked toward the hobo standing next to the burning garbage can. He got the pill bottle out of his pocket and tossed it in the fire. Watching the plastic melt away, turning into smelly gases, I could almost feel it burning my lungs, giving me a headache. Damn, that's good. The hobo looked at the kid as if he were crazy, moving over to the other side of the fire. I gazed into the flames watching them dance, seeing smooth movements of the flames jumping in the air and nipping the hobo's nose. I watched as my younger self hobbled back to the car and the memory ended.

Bodies were starting to pile up, and seeing all their injuries made me want to kick back and have a drink. The blood on my face started to crust over, unlike my hands which were still drenched; I cleaned them off, dipping them in the pool of water. Being in his reality now, feeling what he feels, was unsettling. Seeing what he's made me do. Trying to manipulate me into something I'm not. I can hear him now, "This is quite the theatrics. Look closely in their eyes, and you might be able to see the last thought running through their heads, right before you killed them." Shut up! Shut up! Shut up!

I grabbed the hatchet and began smashing the corpses' skulls in, one by one. I couldn't take their deathly stares anymore. Each swing felt like I was setting them free. A little blood got in my mouth, but that wasn't a huge bother. We just needed to strip judgement from these people. Once finished, the feeling of relief rolled over me. The hatchet was starting to crack, so I stuck it in one of the teenagers' thighs and walked off into the darkness.

The farther I got from the pedestals the darker it got. Several miles away now, it's nearly pitch black. The only sound to be heard is my own footsteps. The feeling of no one around is better than a snow day. No one can bother you; no one can ask you stupid questions, there is freedom here. I'm able to hear my own thoughts and not have that constant need to stab someone.

I could dance right now, and no one would stop to ask me if I was okay.

No one would ask about the strings.

The crowd is the silent killer, it is what makes you feel lonely. Seeing everyone connected to each other, and not being able to find anyone to share your thoughts and feelings with.

I once sat in a coffee shop, sat a table for over three hours, hoping someone would come up to me and say hello. All I got in three hours was a woman asking me if she could steal the chair next to me. I feel like a person could walk right through me and they wouldn't even notice.

It's all his fault. He's been with me too long, making me into something I hate. Making society reject me. If it weren't for him, I could actually feel something, anything. I could be sitting at a table with people I call friends. All he wants is for me to be miserable, right up until the end.

Something tickled my nose, and fell to the dirt. It had a slight glimmer to it. Picking it up off the ground, I discovered that it was a tiny white feather. Not larger than the size of my thumb. A biblical man would think it was a sign of an angel, but I'm not a man who relies on God for answers. I see that as cowardice, as unadulterated fear. People in this world are terrified of everything. It's the product of the mind for survival; when there's an absence of emotional necessity, life itself is an abomination.

But why did this feather fall here? He is a maniac whose own beliefs are anarchy, that need to see the world burn and rise from the ashes of misfortune. This feather, a sign of cowardice, lies here in my hand.

So what terrifies you? What could you possibly be afraid of? Society's rejection? Fear that if I let anyone in, you will be replaced? Whatever it is, it's proof of a blind spot.

I blew the feather off my hand and stood watching it burn up into stardust.

I walked back to the bodies, already feeling less distraught and more perplexed. Seeing the old man's head bashed in felt more palatable now, knowing I'm not defenseless.

I need to get in his skin, know his mindset, somehow become him. I got down and smothered the old man's corpse, wrapping my arms and legs around it, squeezing the juice out of every hole. Burrowing my head into its shoulder, letting my breath warm his nose while his cheeks rested on the cold dirt. There was a feeling of harmony around me in the air. It felt like slow dance. No one around to dull out judgement. I didn't want to let go. I just wanted to suffocate in the arms of this wrinkled corpse, and yet there were more pedestals waiting, with more weapons.

Pulling myself up, I went for the bat. A young couple appeared in front of me. They looked to be dressed for a romantic date, a night out. That little glimmer when their eyes met was priceless. The young man grabbed onto her hips and pulled her near, holding her close. She blushed and wrapped her hands behind his back. Licking his lips, with one hand he brushed her hair back; the other moved down from her waist. He slowly leaned. The girl was standing on her tippy-toes. They both closed their eyes. Time slowed down. Seconds felt like minutes. Seeing this eternity of waiting for their lips to meet, it was fascinating, seeing all the subtle details. The lipstick she wore. The gum he was chewing. The moment felt devastatingly beautiful.

Torqueing my hips, and pulling the bat back, I swung it hard. The man's knee made a loud pop, with a small undertone crackle. He fell to the ground. I wasn't able to hear his screams over the girl's deathly cry. The music to my ears sadly disappeared after I made her head a baseball. And what do you know, it's a home run. Back to the cripple, I caught him crawling away. The bat was still hungry, so I let it have a few more bites before I called it off, poor sap.

It took a second until the liquid mercury spread. What secrets did this puddle hold? A younger me, fifteen years ago to be exact, was sitting in an old apartment. I think it was around the time I started college. Oxy, coke, and everything else fun was spread out across the room. My favorite bong stood on the coffee table. A revolver was pointed to my head. Shifting positions, I held it so I was swallowing the barrel. Pulled it out, put it back in. I changed it so the bullet would come under my chin and out the top.

"What is the point of all of this?"

"What's the point? I don't want to be here anymore."

"So, why are you doing this?"

"I told you. I have no one. As far as the world is concerned, I'm a ghost in the wind. Hovering from place to place."

"But why? Do you even realize the people you are going to hurt, because of your selfishness?"

"What people? The only people who care for me is the voice in my head!"

"Your family. Your mother. She means nothing to you? Your pettiness shouldn't have to hurt the ones who care for you, even if they mean nothing to you."

"All my life, I have been following what everyone else wants. Putting my needs aside to help others. And yet I don't deserve this one thing?"

"No, you don't, because this is bigger than you. You can pout and complain. But death does not deserve you."

134

"Stop it! Stop lying to me. I am nothing. I am just a waste of space! Let me go."

"If you truly think that, then do it. Let everyone think you are a coward. Ruin everyone's lives. Let them feel the pain knowing they can't have you anymore, that they didn't save you. Let them mourn over the avoidable misery that your greedy mind just couldn't manage."

"I don't want to hurt anyone. I just... the pain... it hurts so much. Too much."

"And you killing yourself will solve the problem? I care about our family. Don't do this."

"You're a voice in my head. Constantly telling me no. You can't control me."

"You're right. Kill yourself. Do it, I can't stop you, but if you at any point cared about me, then you will wait until your family is gone. Your mother. Wait until she's passed. Don't make her suffer."

The memory faded. There is nothing crueler, really, than the reminder of being alone in the universe. Not a day goes by that I don't dream of ending it all. I've thought of countless ways to kill myself. Waiting to laugh in his face when it all ends. When I finally win. A quick death, not wanting to hear his insensitive blabbering. I lay there for a while, closed my eyes, and daydreamed about achieving that pure moment.

9: The Upcoming

SEASONS CHANGED, THE SKY TURNED GRAY, snow has fallen, and the frost has spread like a plague. Basically my psyche coming to life.

With the comfort of a pay bump, I was able to get some new headphones. I always hated it when other people could hear my music playing, snooping into other people's business. My past medical records and psychological evaluations covered my desk. Several books on fear were scattered around the room. I was jotting down thoughts and ideas, trying to figure out who or what he is afraid of. I even went as far as looking over my old high school yearbook, scanning the very few signatures and comments that were written in it: "Have a great summer" "Stay Cool" "Try not to have any more mental breakdowns." Funny, that one. Not.

There was a knock at the door, but I didn't initially notice over the music playing. It was my receptionist, and she tried getting my attention several times. Finally I felt a tap on my shoulder, and jumped in my chair. Without thinking, I grabbed the letter opener, and was half a second away from stabbing her in the abdomen. Now pissed, I paused my music.

"What?!" I stared down at the desk, trying not to make eye contact.

"Sorry. You have a meeting in ten minutes." She backed away.

"Thank you." I waved her off.

I grabbed the notes off my desk and shoved them into the top drawer. Resuming my headphones music, I walked over and stood in front of my office window, gazing over my view of the small, little people. Watching them live their worthless little lives. It always puzzled me how people didn't see logic. Give a man a gun, and there is anarchy. Give an army a feather, and their society is protected. What a joke.

Walking into the meeting, I saw there were about twelve or fifteen people sitting at a table looking just as profession and well dressed as I do. One of them wore a pink tie. I always found it hard to pull off pink, not because it's a feminine color, it just doesn't match my skin tone. I would never say it to him, but I was a little jealous to see someone else pull it off when I can't. I sat next to the boss. She wore a black pantsuit with a white blouse, but it wasn't a ladies' blouse, it was the type a pirate might wear; I never understood why that was so popular. The man in the pink tie was speaking.

"All right, now that everyone is here" as he glared at me "I need to see some numbers. Jason, how do our offshore factories look?"

"Right now, with the steel tariff in effect, we have lost about seven percent of production," a man a few chairs over to my left said.

"Get hold of Alex, see if you can find a way to work around this. Bill, has China come to an agreement on the KT project yet?"

"China has yet to respond to the agreement. They still have a week left until anything can be finalized."

"Get them on the phone now, and tell them that if they don't give us an answer by tomorrow, we will be taking our business elsewhere."

"Sir, it's the middle of the night there. There's no one-"

"I don't give a shit if it's the middle of the night. Tell them now or you're fired."

I laughed at Bill under my breath. Apparently it was too loud, because the meeting guy in charge looked at me as if I were his next victim. "Oh, Mr. Squeaky here has something to say. Well?"

Unlike the rest of these worm-for-brains losers, I was not scared of this dickhead.

"Huh," I started, "well the stock has been depleting from 573 to 521 the past month. If you look at the news, you would see that the corporation has been linked to several oil spills across the Pacific Ocean. If you want the public to view us as something more than a money-greedy corporation, put on a big charity event for something that sounds sad, you know, like 'stop school shootings.' You'll be the belle of the ball."

"And where are we going to put on this fabulous charity ball?" he asked.

"It's a five-billion-dollar company, I think there's some wiggle room to help you not look like an ass."

"Why don't I just fire you?" His voice rose. "Would that be enough wiggle room?"

"You could," I told him, "but then all you would have left is a bunch of self-consumed narcissists who would love to fuck you over in your sleep."

Everyone at the table was silent. Not a single person moved a muscle. Not even an awkward cough.

The boss looked at me, most likely waiting for an apology. I looked him square in the face, opened my mouth, and inserted a double-stuff Oreo. The crunching, with my lips parted on purpose, made an echo. Parched, I grabbed one of the bottled waters from the center of the table. Twisting the lid off and taking a gulp, I grabbed for another Oreo.

"Where are we with liquidating the Philips branch?" diving back into safe waters, the dickhead pretended our little exchange had never happened.

I zoned out the rest of the meeting. By the time it ended, the time was 1:30 p.m. My stomach growled. Flicking on my headphones music, I threw on my speckled gray overcoat.

The snowfall now was heavy, and the icy wind made it hurt to open my eyes. Finally, I could walk where I belonged, down the street of gold. Old women wore big fur coats and carried tiny disgusting dogs. Men walked with the splotch-less boots, wearing Rolexes like they were toys from a kid's meal. They carried themselves like gods. They and I both knew better.

I walked past restaurants, some where the tabs are larger than some people's annual wages. There was one restaurant I spotted that had an especially elegant outer entrance. Walking inside, I saw the lights were dimmed, but each table had a candle, making the room feel debonair and classy. The hostess stood at a polished lectern with a shiny black striped blouse matching her pants. She mouthed something, but I wasn't about to make the effort in stopping my music to hear her speak.

"Table for one," I said, talking over my music.

She me led to a table in the center of the room. The chairs were nice, fine oak wood frames with black leather seats and backs. The seat cushion wasn't terrible, but I was sitting on a spring, and it wasn't like sinking into a pillow. I counted five fat cats gorging on their meats, while their escorts daintily pushed around their salads.

The bartender's tip jar was nearly full of large bills. That wasn't surprising though; nearly every employee here looked like a supermodel. A woman in her late forties sat at the bar eyeing a young blond man with a chiseled jaw. She waved the barkeep over to her, said something and put a hundred-dollar bill in the tip jar. The barkeep looked at her, then at the young man, then back at her. She handed him something. The barkeep walked off and started making a drink. He picked up a large spherical ice cube with metal tongs and set it in a glass. He got a bottle from the top shelf on the backbar and slid it over to the blond man seated at the bar, who looked at the woman, raised the glass, and gave a little nod.

Someone tapped me on my shoulder. Once again, I reached for a knife. I turned around and saw the waiter. I didn't see a point in pausing my music yet; I already knew what he was going to ask and what I'd order.

"I want the broiled halibut with light coating of pesto cream sauce, and a side of roasted brussels sprouts seasoned with olive oil and pepper. If I see one burnt brussels sprout, I will send it back. If the halibut is dry, I will send it back. Do anything else to it that I didn't ask for, I will send it back."

The waiter scribbled a note. "To drink I would like a glass of red wine, and no, I don't know what kind I want. I trust you have a fine palate, so you can pick for me. Now I do realize that you yourself are not the cook, and you have no control over how my food is made. But you will be tipped on your performance and how much you annoy me, and whether or not you will refill water – which I still haven't received – and how fast you get me my drinks. If I find that your service is adequate, then you will be well compensated for your services. Note that I do not want you to constantly be running to my table to check on me. You see these earbuds? This means I don't want to be disturbed. So come over here only when asked. Nod if you understand me."

He nodded, eyes wide, and rushed off. Less than a minute later, he reappeared with a glass of wine and an icewater. He stood there as I judged his choice. Good enough, I thought, and I waved him off.

While waiting for my food, I pulled paper and pencil from my inner blazer pocket. There is an endless imagination with a blank canvas. It can be frustrating, overwhelming to know exactly what you want, but without the means to accomplish it, lacking the willpower to do what you want or need. I started scribbling, shading, drawing lines, precise movements, making sure that I didn't screw up. I dipped my fingers in the wine and let a couple droplets fall on the paper. Grabbing a napkin, I cleaned off my hands.

Food had arrived. I snapped my fingers and the waiter quickly brought me another wine. He grabbed my empty glass and hurried off. He wasted no time in catering to my needs, and the food was spectacular. Steam rose from the halibut as I forked into it. It offered just a slight taste of lemon and garlic, tiptoeing across my tastebuds, and was still tender and moist. Knowing another living being had died to give me this solitude, it was well worth it. Trying the sprouts, they were perfectly charred. They didn't leave the taste of charcoal or kitchen grill in my mouth. The black pepper danced around my tongue and the choreography was spectacular. The simplicity of the meal is what made it nearly perfect. There were no exaggerated explosions, no overpowering spices. It was phenomenal.

I flipped the piece of paper over and resumed my search for the answer. But now I was drawing a blank. Nothing more came to mind. The tip of the pencil broke, poofing pencil lead dust across the tablecloth. I threw the pencil across the room and hit an old man in the back of the head.

I snapped my waiter over.

"Check."

He had my respect. I handed him a hundred-dollar bill. In just a minute my change came back. I pulled him in close, our faces only a few inches apart, and I went into my wallet again. I pulled out a fifty-dollar bill.

I grabbed the young man's face. "Say Ah," I told him, and I placed the bill between his teeth.

"You can leave now." He walked away looking satisfied.

I looked at my drawing one last time, seeing my terrible creation. A man screaming, bleeding tears.

My focus turned back toward the bar. It looked like the bartender was cleaning out some cups, and down the bar from him, I could see another employee helping the middle-aged woman carry out the unconscious blond guy she'd bought a drink for. Good luck to you, sir.

I walked out the door, snow hitting my eyes again. Hardly any light shone through the heavy clouds. The time on the bank sign said 3:49 p.m. and I could feel the frost cut my cheek. I paused to consider.

Work was a miserable place, seeing strangers who only want to tear me down. My only friend is an asshole who never wants to be around me. To top it off, my new boss is a power-crazed freak.

The gym seemed a fair option. The floor would be empty, with no one around to bother me.

When I got there I grinned, pleased that my estimate of zero people was correct. I grabbed a sledgehammer off the wall and went for the tire. It was old and ragged, covered in bruises and unhealed scars. It looked sad, hanging here all alone, an outcast among the rest of the equipment.

Feeling the wood slide through my fingers, slamming the rubber. Every swing felt like a little fracture of hope breaking free. Sweat built up over my forehead, getting under my eyes. *Harder*, I told myself. The sting was good, leaving my arms vibrating, paralyzed, forcing me to stay focused. Push through the pain. Keep going. Hearing the bash as the hammer broke the tire's skull, watching as it begged for mercy.

The music came to a halt. It was a gym employee. "Sorry, but you're being kind of loud, and other people are starting to complain."

Looking back around, I saw the room was still quite empty. What the fuck? Before I could start in on him, he walked off.

Asshole.

The showers were always a good place to empty my mind, and turning the nozzle far right, the water slowly dripped, then a second later it became a pressurized burn. Meat was falling off the bone. The nerves were scalded to the point where pain was nothing more than a pinch on the cheek. Closing my

143

eyes, I imagined red flowing down my leg and sucked down the drain. Bringing my head up, the water sprayed my face. It was hard to control my breathing. The insides of my eyes started to melt back into my skull. After a minute I couldn't take it anymore, and I backed away from the water and fell to the floor.

I got out of the shower dripping wet. I walked back to the locker room area, where there were mirrors at the end of each row of lockers. I assumed these were for self-indulgence, to look in the mirror and flex, admiring the perfection of the human body. For other guys, that is – all I saw was a pig, snorting and squealing. Hair running frantic across my face. Thousands of bumps and ridges covered the skin. Bloodshot eyes. Dark deep circles.

I made the face of a dragon and hissed at my reflection like a cat. All the folds and wrinkles came to life, showing the beast that lies within.

I had a change of clothing in a locker. A pair of black trousers, white button-down shirt, a silver tie and black vest. With the complement of my dress overcoat, it was fair. The only annoyance was that it felt a bit loose.

The snowfall had picked up by the time I hit the street. Fewer people now walked the sidewalks. Music drowned out the traffic, but not the profound signals the drivers made at one another. The streets were dusted white.

I'm tired of the same old. I need something to pique my interest. Something new. Something like... like the liquor store across the street. Walking in, I thought it smelled of a man who loved to test his own products plus burnt cigars. The owner sat behind the register reading the local newspaper. He flipped the page, and I saw there was an article on the front headlined "Killer Clown Still on the Loose." This obese pig here had obviously never heard of self-preservation. Just looking at him, it was obvious he had no sense of direction or design. From the ceiling to the floor, everything was fine-crafted wood, from the smooth cubicles holding select bottled wine, to the hand-crafted shelves displaying whiskeys and rums. I felt like a kid in the candy store. Strolling through, I saw again the bottle of a pirate walking the plank. I grabbed the large bottle. Admiring the design, though, I noticed something irked my brain. Like I've been here before.

Doesn't matter.

"Ahem," trying to get the owner's attention.

He looked up and froze. After a few seconds there was still no response. I waved and snapped my fingers at him. The idiot was then stupid enough to pull a shotgun on me.

"Get out! Get the fuck out of my store!" he took a couple steps toward me.

I really didn't feel like arguing with this maniac.

"Okay," I tried, "Listen, all I want to do is buy this bottle, no need to overreact."

He lifted the shotgun to his shoulder.

"All right, well I can't say it's been a pleasure doing business with you." On my way out of the store, paused long enough to snag a beer out of the cooler.

"Drop it!" he barked. Drama queen.

"Shoot me!" I twisted off the beer's cap and flicked it into the trashcan on my way out.

I walked fast and quickly finished the beer, tossing it into a dumpster on my way by. The broken glass would soon be covered up by the falling snow. Seeing a stranger ready to blow a hole in my head was definitely the highlight of my day. Too chicken to pull the trigger though, that was somewhat annoying.

As I walked down the street, minding my own business, some jerk actually decided to trip me. I stumbled hard but didn't go down, and turning back around, I saw it was the bum from a few months ago begging at that stoplight, now begging from an appliance-sized cardboard box covered in blankets.

I paused my music.

"Hey, you're the ... that guy. Yeah, you're that bum who sits next to the traffic every day." I crouched down to match his eye level.

He looked at me confused.

"Enlighten me," I said. "Why do you stand out here every day, letting weather control your where and when you sleep?"

"What?"

"Well, you see, you live outside, where it's currently snowing. So tell me, why?"

"Why what."

"Holy shit, do you not speak English? Why don't you just go and get a job?"

"Um-I-I-uh ..."

"Read my lips. I assume you can read, right? Why don't you get a job?"

"I um, ahh, well ..."

"You know what, just forget that. I'm going to give you something far better than money."

146

"You got coke?" the guy looked hopeful.

"No."

"Bath salts?"

"No, but I like your style. No, I'm going to give you advice." I edged in close, letting my breath moisten his eyeglasses. "Shave the beard and lose the ugly mole, and maybe you'll be worth looking at."

A couple doors down was a gun store. The inside smelled of meat and cheese, like someone had just finished a sandwich, with a hint of old pipe smoke. Guns covered the walls and lined the display shelves: rifles, shotguns, revolvers, semi-automatics, even a small cannon. Stands were set up around the store holding ammunition and other related supplies. My index and middle finger slid across the glass counter, leaving behind a fingerprint streak. The handguns in the case attracted my eye. So small, yet so lethal.

"Can I help you with anything?" the hillbilly behind the counter asked.

"Ah yeah, can I see that one?" pointing at a pistol with black grips and a shiny chrome slide.

"Ah, a Ruger fan?"

Just holding it felt nice, and my index finger rubbed against the trigger guard, like having the power to make a politician kneel. Looking down the sights, aiming at the floor, I felt powerful. I paused, and shuffled my music. Then I took a deep breath, closed my eyes, and let the music flow through me. Twisting and jumping, leaping from corner to corner of the gun case, another customer warned "Watch it!" and I retaliated by aiming and firing at him. Gunfire exploded across the room as I took each of the customers out one by one. The owner behind the counter pulled his own gun – a long-barreled big revolver, and fired at me. A bullet zinged past my shoulder as I danced across the room. Moving toward the door with my one bullet left, I aimed right at the owner's face, just as a bullet thumped through my chest. I fell to the floor with a smile on my face. Exhaling, I opened my eyes.

"I'll take it."

Exiting the store, I shoved the pistol down the back of my pants.

The street was now empty, and hardly any cars were parked along its sides. The snow started to feel more like hail. I found myself at a loss. There was nothing to do.

That bartender, he had seemed like an interesting character. Walking back into the restaurant, I saw him scrubbing down his station.

"Just one?" a different hostess asked me.

The bartender had an ugly smile.

"Sir?" the hostess still tried to get my attention.

"None." I walked past her.

The barstools were uncomfortable to sit on. There was another man sitting a few seats down from me, breaking open peanut shells.

Pausing my music to look over the drink menu, I saw it was filled with elaborate and fancy cocktails.

"What can I get you?" the barkeep asked.

"A knife and someone who needs to be taught a lesson. Please and thank you. Oh, and some peanuts if you have any," It said.

"Dealer's choice."

"Dark 'n' Stormy?"

"Sure."

Swiveling the stool back, I saw the restaurant was mostly empty now. A few business-suited men sat at a round table. Laughing. Laughing and drinking. "Any special occasion?" he was pouring ginger beer over my iced rum.

"What's with all the questions? Mind your own business, or don't. I wonder what the insides of his eyeballs look like."

"Eh, just looking to take the edge off. The voice in my head is driving me insane."

"What a nice thing to say. I'm blushing ..."

"I get it," said the bartender, squeezing a lime wedge over my drink.

"I sincerely doubt that," It commented.

"Yeah," said I, looking around the room. Too nice a place for a bouncer. No security, just waiters and busboys and that hostess.

"Haven't seen you around here before." He set a bowl of peanuts by my coaster.

I swiveled back around and sipped my drink. It wasn't bad, though he was a little light on the rum.

"What do you think?" he asked.

"Could use some more rum."

He didn't respond.

"You ever get creeps in here?"

"More often than not," he muttered. Now he was reluctant to talk to me.

"Any interesting stories?" I asked, dropping a ten in his tip jar.

"Well, one time there was this guy who sat right where you were sitting. I asked him what he wanted. He didn't really seem to care, but after one sip, he critiques the drink and says there isn't enough rum in it."

"Sounds fun," I said.

"Not really. I mean it beats seeing the same oversized fat cats in here every day."

"Meh, not wrong," I told him.

"So, what do you do, something that makes my paycheck look like petty change?"

"Me? I work with the mentally disabled." I took another drink.

"Oh we're lying now, I see." It just had to get into the conversation.

"Oh, so you deal with retards then?" asked the bartender.

"Um, not exactly, and ah, we don't say that." I was now a little pissed.

"You should kill him," I heard.

"Doing okay?" he asked, not really caring, cleaning off the bar.

"You ever steal any drinks?" I asked him.

"Not really, enough people around here like to buy my drinks to the point where I'm just constantly buzzed."

"Fun." I said, with little enthusiasm, looking at the ice in my drink.

"Yeah, I mean there are some days where I've gotten so drunk I forget I'm even working, but I've got to make tips somehow, you know."

"Sure. So... that woman who was here earlier. She a good tipper?"

He looked at me confused. "I get a lot of women coming by. You need to be more specific."

"Remember, the one that bribed you to slip something into that blond guy's drink."

"Oh, interesting. Look to see if there's anything to stab him with."

"Shut up," I sharply whispered at him.

The pretty-boy smile faded quickly. "I don't know what you're talking about."

"Sure you do. Tell me, is she one of your regulars, or was that just like a onetime thing?" I finished off my drink.

"I think it's time for you to go," he said, in a barely threatening tone. He made a subtle gesture at a co-worker, a waiter, at the back of the room.

I subtly placed the gun on the bar.

He pointed his friend off. "What do you want?"

"Well, you still haven't answered my question," trying to keep my emotions in check.

"What?"

"What is it with everyone today! Umm! Ehhhh! What! Am I not speaking clearly? Is it my enunciation? Was that woman a regular or not."

"W-why does it matter?"

I cocked the gun.

"Careful, look around for cameras." ... as if I need a warning.

"Wow ... Okay, okay. She's a regular. Comes in once or twice a week."

"And do you know where she lives?"

"Dude come on, I'm just a bartender!"

I leaned over the bar, grabbed him by his shirt, and yanked him up against the bar in front of me, the barrel aimed right between his eyes.

"You know, I'm trying not to lose my temper here, and you're really not helping."

He looked at the other man across the bar.

"Hey, don't look at him! He doesn't need any help. Look at me. The address?"

"Yeah, yeah, I think I know it." He reached under the counter to grab something.

I shoved the gun into his eye.

"Relax! Relax! Relax! Just grabbing pen and paper."

He wrote down an address on a napkin and handed it to me.

"If you're lying to me, your last drink will be a bullet. You understand?"

He nodded.

"You have a little smudge on your lip," I calmly said, wiping it off.

I let him go. He jumped away and hit the back bar.

The guy at the other end of the bar was looking at me, still cracking shells and eating peanuts. He looked at me and looked at the gun. Then he went back to minding his own business.

I left a twenty on the bar and headed for the door.

"Pulling a gun on a random stranger... doesn't seem like your usually well-mannered self," said my constant companion. "May I suggest the next time you take him out back, and leave him for the rats to feast on."

"No."

"You always leave too soon." It said, disappointed.

"Bite me."

I walked back to my apartment, planning my groundwork to deal with a different monster. An almost perfect plan needs a clear mind, and I've found the best way to do that is by drinking. Luckily, my liquor cabinet is never empty. I poured myself a glass of apple pie moonshine. The cinnamon was mouthwatering, but it kicked like a horse. Three drinks in and I'm numb, head to toe.

The room was boiling; I changed into my birthday suit. The jittery tingle faded to a calming numb, and every once in a while I wiped nonexistent drool from my lip. My old yet voguish leather burgundy couch was a fine place to just lie back and watch TV. Occasionally I hit my hand against the coffee table just to feel the pain, but it was strange not having an opinion on it. The most memorable thing about being intoxicated was fantasizing a reflection of me gripping my face and screaming "Kill me! Kill me!" I was incapable of feeling pain or sorrow. It was a state of neither happy nor sad, depressed or excited, just colorless.

Stand up was a challenge. Taking one step was a whole different game. My legs were like wooden sticks. The best bet was to waddle like a penguin. Sadly, that only worked for three steps, after which I landed on my face. Getting up was not much of an option. Rolling onto my back, now that was plausible. First priority, getting another drink. Using all my strength, I butt-scooted to the kitchen. Ready men? Scoot! Scoot! Scoot! My head made a thud against the lower cabinet doors.

"Come here, bottle. Give me some of your juice," I said blindly, reaching for the moonshine. It felt swinish to drink straight from the bottle, but it definitely cut out the middleman, and saved time. A few more drinks in, and black out.

10: Bread and Butter

THE SNOWFALL HAD STOPPED, and a window must've been open, because a breeze blew around the room riffling papers and fabric. There was a thin layer of frost building up atop my skin. My eyelids were frozen shut.

My stomach growled; time to go to my somewhat-tolerable but not so happy place. The black silk apron tied itself around my waist. Turning the faucet to a warm 102 degrees, I wet my hands, followed by lathering them in soap, scrubbing between every wrinkle and crevice for twenty seconds, scratching my palms to get soap under the nails. Again rinsing, drying off with a towel hanging on the stand next to the sink.

When preparing breakfast, the first thing was to cut red potatoes into fourths, drizzling them in olive oil, adding in some homegrown minced garlic. While the potatoes were baking, ice cold champagne was waiting to be stirred with freshly squeezed orange juice to make the mimosa. When first making orange juice, it was challenging. Over time it gets easier to strangle the fruit, squeezing out every last drop. I spooned out the guts into a cup, drowning it in water. Then came straining the pulp, combining the water and juice into one cup, and I tossed the pulp away. Finally, the champagne at a strong ratio of 3:1, to keep the mind in a constant hazed state.

Hearing the crack of the delicate egg shells breaking was appealing. Grinding the salt and pepper onto the eggs reminded me of ash falling from the sky. The goo turned white. In flipping the eggs over one at a time, I saw one of the yolks break. It was ugly, watching the yolk bleed out of the unborn corpse. There is no room for imperfections when making food. The egg founds its place in the trash, where it belonged. The potatoes were done.

The apron didn't want to leave my chest, and arguing was pointless. The dining room patiently waited for my presence. Scooping the minced garlic potatoes and eggs onto the china, pouring the mimosa mixture into its proper glass, I took my seat at the table. Decapitating the eggs and stabbing potatoes was timeless. The mimosa took the edge off, preparing the mind and body to face reality.

After finishing breakfast, the dishes floated into the kitchen sink. The yellow rubber gloves slid over my fingers. A blue sponge jumped into my hands, as hot water flowed down the drain. Bubbles burst out of the sponge. I scrubbed the pan, getting rid of the stuck-on yolk from my failure. The water washed away the rest of the grease, leaving behind a shine. A separate towel was used to dry the dishes. Afterwards, the pan found its way back to its personal standing rack in the cupboard. The baking sheet needed to be wiped to get rid of the olive oil. The rest of the dishes cleaned themselves.

Time for the morning routine, scrubbing the scum off my body, followed by the teeth. Walking into the closet, it felt like a sweater vest day. Throwing on a white long-sleeve shirt, I picked an ivory-colored tie with a crosshatch design, and over that was the black sweater vest; pulling it all together was a midnight-shade blazer and pants. When I walk outside, I want people to hate me for how much better I look than they do.

So, it was time to show off the black chukka boots. My reflection looked like a stone-cold killer, giving me a little wink, as if to say "Hello hot shit."

Time sped up, and I found myself standing in front of my office door. My office chair was ugly. It belonged with the slum, and to the slum it shall go. The chair flew out the window, making a new natural air conditioner. I was already done with today, and the couch in the corner of my office looked very comfortable. Lying down to take a nap, I watched as a ten-foot-tall teddy bear, holding several boxes of double-stuffed Oreos, stared me down from the opposite side of the room.

"What are you looking at?" I finally asked it.

Ted Bear said nothing.

"You think you're better than me? You're cotton fluff that looks like something a street corner hobo would own."

The bear's head fell to the side.

"Yeah, that's what I thought."

The room was getting cold, and it was impossible to take a nap with the bear eyeing me like a hot piece of meat, so the next best option was to go for a power walk. My
156

receptionist wasn't sitting at her desk. How rude. As a form of discipline, all her knickknacks and desk computer kissed the ground.

The receptionist in the next desk over cheered me on. "Bravo! Magnificent!" he clapped. "Encore! Encore!"

An encore he wanted, an encore he shall get. I grabbed his bobblehead and threw it at the wall. The head broke off smacking another of the office incompetents in the head. What do we have in the breakroom? A bunch of plastic utensils, stale doughnuts, and a half-eaten bagel. Great. Peering in the fridge, I saw there was a gallon-sized bag filled with baby carrots. Fascinating. Chomping down on one of them, I thought there has never been a better tasting carrot to have ever lived. It was sweet and yet bitter; the taste held a butter flavor, but had none on it. No one deserves these carrots more than I do. I stole the bag and headed down to my old work space. The elevator was playing Barry Manilow. The old office smelt of cat piss; how suiting. Phil immediately saw me.

"Dude!" he jumped from a cubicle aiming to give me a big hug.

Right before he could tackle me, Linda came around the corner, saw me, and knocked him on his ass instead.

"Lib!" she squealed, latching onto me.

Her cold fingers felt like insects crawling over my skin, trying to lay their eggs in the dark corners of my body. My one free arm was able to get some leverage by pushing in her face. My fingers got caught in her mouth, covered in saliva. After a few seconds of eye gouging, she broke away.

"Oh my gosh! How are you? It's been like forever!" she brushed her hair back, showing off her forehead.

"Um, good I guess."

"You totally like have to tell me everything!" she went to latch onto me again.

Phil pushed her aside to get a word in.

"Bro! Bro! We totally need to go and get a drink right now!" he said, grabbing my face.

What is it with people trying to touch me?

"Er-uh, sure," not thinking.

"'Ey, what's with the bag, bro?"

His voice really started to irritate me. The only way to shut him up was to shove a handful of carrots down his throat. He started to turn blue as he chewed and chomped on the sweet carrots. There was a good minute of loud annoying crunching before he was gasping for air. He tried to speak again, but was forced to choke down more carrots. Linda also attempted to speak, but I covered her big mouth before she could make another sound. She took the hint and took a few carrots.

The best thing to do, I decided, was to walk away, screw the ol' cubicle. Phil caught up with me, and started to talk about a strip club he'd been to the night before, telling me how all the "chicks" there loved him. Running was no longer an option; he would follow me off a cliff. Then where would I be, piss me off, hearing him talk about his narcissistic self in hell. The only choice left was to take a seat on top of the table in the back, and let him blabber on.

At some point his voice sounded like TV buzz. With a bag full of carrots, there was only one thing left to do, throw them at the underlings. Phil joined in, still talking about who knows what. A carrot landed in Linda's blouse. She laughed, jumping up and down, showing off her cleavage. One of the carrots hit an underling in the eye, and he freaked out.

"Hey! Watch it, asshole!" the underling rudely shouted.

"Shut up."

"I will fuck you up, man!" he said, standing up and walking out of his cubicle.

"Go ahead, I don't give a shit," letting the joke play out.

"Oh, Mr. Corporate thinks he's better than the rest of us. You don't even deserve that job, you fucking retard!"

That struck a nerve.

"The fuck you just say?" I marched over to him. There were a lot of pens around the room. A lot of things to stab him with.

"You don't deserve to be a superstar, you fuckin' reta-" I slapped him in the face before he could finish his sentence.

I got up close, so he wouldn't miss a single word.

"Now listen here you piece of shit, I will happily take you to the bathroom and break that fucking jaw of yours. Not before I shove those scissors up your ass, and then use them to cut off that oversized tongue. Next, I would not only fire you, but also take away your severance package, leaving you with nothing. Then your wife will accept the fact that she married a fucking loser, that's when I step in and fuck her too. Don't worry, when she files for divorce, I'll make sure she gets everything. The house, the money, even the clothes off your back, and you'll be stuck with those kids. And while you're crying yourself to sleep in your cardboard box, I'll be making sweet, sweet, love to some other bitch in Jamaica, because your wife must truly look God-awful if she married the likes of you."

He stood there speechless.

I walked away.

Taking my seat back at the table, Phil acted like nothing had happened. My body was flowing with adrenaline, feeling the urge to punch something. Phil nudged my shoulder trying to get my attention.

"Bro, so can we?"

"What?" I turned on him, not wanting to listen to him at this moment, or ever.

"If there is any money left in the budget at the end of the quarter, can we spend it on strippers and coke?"

"Uh, sure, whatever," still not giving him my full attention.

"Sweet!" he squealed like a little girl. "Ey, speaking of sweets, I got you something." He handed me a box Oreos.

"I'm not a fan."

The bag of carrots was empty. Fun's over. Time to go back to the office and find peaceful seclusion. The elevator doors slid open, playing Sex & Drug & Rock & Roll by Ian Dury. A song that had no meaning behind it, straight to the point, and is very good indeed. Phil was sprinting toward the elevator doors.

"Come on! Come on! Come on!!" he stood repeatedly pressing the close-door button.

He looked up at me. "You still haven't shown me your new fancy office."

"Oh yeah, sure," now I was pissed off at the elevator gods.

"Bro, this song's my jam," he said, rocking out to the tune.

"Meh, it's okay." I leaned against the side of the elevator.

161

We stood there in silence as the music played.

"Why can't you be more like this?" I asked out loud.

"Like what?" Phil said, confused as usual.

"Never mind."

The elevator doors opened again. I led Phil to my office.

"Wow bro, this place is awesome, and that chick outside, shocking!"

"You mean my receptionist? She just turned seventeen."

That was a lie, she was actually twenty-four.

"Ey, don't matter to me. You'll see, I'll have her blowing my flute in no time," he said, grinding the air.

Sometimes I wonder, would the world be better if Phil wasn't around. I should just kill him and be done with it. "That's a new one," I told him. "You like it?"

"If you call demonizing one of the purest harmonistic instruments, titling it as something as odious as one's phallus, then yes, I enjoyed it." I said, lifting the painting off the wall to reveal a safe.

"Nice!" he said, taking pride in his disrespectful linguistics.

The safe involved a four-digit code.

"Turn around," I told him, covering up the keypad.

3-8-2-5

The safe popped open, revealing two glasses and a bottle of 12-year-old scotch. This felt odd, leaning on the side of creepy.

"Why don't you uh, why don't you go and get some uh... ice." I looked at Phil and waved my hand, expecting him to leave.

"Yeah sure." he said, and he walked out.

The last time I shared a drink... This is not something I can or will be comfortable with. The feeling of sharing a meal, sipping on refreshments, finding that attachment amongst others – it's like reopening a scar and watching it bleed out onto the carpet. To share a drink is to lay it all out there, and let others judge you at your most vulnerable.

There was a gentle knock at the door.

"Come in."

"Hey-O, Iceman is in the house!" Phil cheerfully jumped in.

He had an ice bucket and little tongs, and the bucket was full. I held both the glasses out, and Phil used the tongs to drop a few cubes into each of them. Handing one of the glasses to Phil, I poured myself a fair amount of scotch. Phil snatched the bottle and poured a drink that was larger than mine. Unacceptable. He pulled the drink to his lips. "Wait!"

Phil paused before a single drop could touch his tongue. The glass whispered to me, "He doesn't deserve me."

"Can I see your glass for just one second?" and I took the glass from his hand.

It took five gulps and a killer burn, but I finished the drink.

Phil looked at me baffled. "Are you okay?"

"I'm fine," I said, finishing my own glass.

"You sure?"

"You ask me again, and I'll make those meatballs you call nipples your new eyeballs."

Phil started his clubbing tales, and I knew if I didn't cut him off, an invite would be part of the story.

"Actually, I'm not feeling so good."

"Okay," he said, "then I'll catch you later, I guess." He left.

Finally.

My leather swivel chair looked very comfortable. I sat. This is true relaxation. Phil's gift of packaged Oreos now was eyeing me. Using the ice tongs to pluck an Oreo, I dipped it in the scotch. The flavor was adequate. Not bad.

The hole in the wall was daring. It would be priceless to follow gravity. Time would slow down, and I might be able to find enjoyment in the last few moments of my life. Sticking my head out the window, the wind flowed through my hair. It was strong wind, with bits of ice flakes slashing my cheeks. An interesting idea popped into my head. Let's throw the bottle out the window, and see if it hits anyone. Getting a good grip on the neck, I sent it soaring across the sky. I licked the frosting part of the Oreo while watching the bottle sail down. It targeted a crowd of unfortunate bastards. Come on, baby, show me something good. And it's a, it's a... failure. The bottle landed few yards too soon.

Damn it.

As a way to apologize, I tossed them what was left of the package of Oreos.

Time was going by too slowly. A stack of mail littered my desk. Instead of being responsible, I pulled out the desk drawer to dump it with the rest of the trash. The gun and the note jumped into my hands.

Why not, I thought, pointing a gun at the weak does sound amusing, and her apartment isn't too far away. Stuffing a few of the janitor's latex gloves in my pocket, the journey began.

Outside the blinding reflection of the snow burned my eyesockets, making it almost impossible to see. Quiet though. No one stood on the corners begging for spare change, no annoying couples trying to show the world how perfect they are, just me and the empty traffic. I felt like dancing, but being a rather solemn person, there was a reputation to uphold.

The building where the woman lived was very disgusting, matching the neighborhood, kinda like my old apartment. The front doors were locked. Looking at the paper again, I saw the name was Sky Taylor.

Sky Taylor, what an interesting name for an ugly soul.

Pressing the button, I heard a voice answer a few seconds later. "Hello?"

"Oh, hi, I forgot my keys inside. Can you punch me in."

"What kind of idiot are you," she said, sounding snobby.

"You going to let me in or not?" The door buzzed. "Thanks."

So, not only is she a rapist, but also an asshole. The elevator was busted. Thirty-three fucking floors. Room 28 H. Her door had an old coat of brown paint chipping off, and the door handle was rusted. I felt fortunate that I'd thought to bring the latex gloves. Snapping a pair on, I knocked on the door. No answer. Again, I knocked.

"Go away!" a voice from the inside yelled.

How rude. It's only appropriate to keep knocking until she finds the decency to say that to my face. Maybe banging will help.

She creeps it open, barely showing her face. "Do you not understand-"

It was a waste of time to let her finish her rambling. Forcing myself in, I saw her place looked very nice. Dramatically unlike the outside – much more like how a person with a six-figure salary would live.

"You can't just barge in here!" She wore a tight black leather bra and skirt to match it.

"Just did." I admired the cleanliness of the room. There was a hallway to my left. Kicking in the first door, I saw it was an office. The next one was just a room with a dirty and rumpled twin bed in the corner. Kicking down the third and final door, I was stunned to see a very elaborate dungeon. There were whips and bloody paddles on the walls, several knives and collars, along with other tools. In the very center was a small metal table, with bondage tools and accoutrements hanging from the ceiling.

"You know, you could really make this place pop it you just added a red or black fur on the walls, or maybe a fiery magenta color. Yeah, definitely a magenta."

"The police are on their way!" she said, walking into the room behind me.

"Don't bullshit me, you called the police when you're hiding all of this shit? I think not. Why don't you just save me the trouble of looking for the boy, and just tell me where he is."

She reached for a paddle.

"Really, you're going to try to fight me? Are you stupid or just blind, because I don't know if you noticed, but I have a fucking gun."

She moved forward anyhow.

"I'm not wasting my time with you." I fired the gun, only grazing her leg.

She fell to the floor screaming.

Then I saw there was another door in the room.

I eased the door open and saw it was him, the man from the bar. Naked and covered in cuts and bruises. He lay on the floor, both his wrists and ankles tied.

"Hey! Hey! Hey buddy," gently tapping his face. "Wake up, I'm gonna get you out of here. Come on, wake up!"

I searched but he had no pulse. On his back were deep lashes, revealing muscle cut so deeply I could almost see the bone. The sight was unbearable. Looking up, I found a display case filled with bags of hair.

My hands were shaking, and the blood drained from my face. I battled with myself to not succumb to the anger. The psychopath in the other room was calling for help. Blood was covering the floor. I went back to her. Dragging her by her hair, I threw her into the closet with the corpse.

"You think this is fun, abusing the innocent!" I forced her to look at the blond guy.

"I'm gonna kill you!" she hissed.

Pressing her face to the ground, I caved in her nose.

I used the butt end of the pistol to knock her out.

The shaking in my knees calmed down, and that left me with a mess to clean up. It would have been so easy to just steal her last breath and leave her to rot. But once the hourglass breaks, so scatters the sand.

Walking carefully back into the dungeon, I saw there were several toys that caught my attention. On the wall, there were several hammers and knives, leather tassel whips; out of all the toys and trinkets in this nightmare, the most compelling was a jar filled with yellow peeps. Seriously.

Back out the way I came, the kitchen actually looked professional, with the counters' top layer of white marble. An island stood front and center along with a tall stainless faucet. The range had an electric stovetop with two ovens, one above and one below. The fridge was like something out of a Syfy movie. You could place your hands on the glass, and it would turn from blurry to clear without needing to open the fridge doors. Inside was a nice bottle of champagne, uncorked yet still full. Just for me. Not the best, but it will do.

Taking a gulp of the chilled champagne, I let the foam run down my chin, leaving behind goosebumps.

Everything in this room was organized in a way so that the eyes don't wander off; different cooking pots and utensils hung from the ceiling and walls. In the corner of the countertop was a bamboo sushi mat with a bowl of avocados. A juicer sat next to a bread box that smelled of sourdough. Opening the box, I found it was indeed a loaf of freshly made sourdough. Grabbing a knife off the wall, and slicing, the crust crackled. Sitting on the other side of the box was a wooden sphere cut in half. Removing the top half of it, I saw what looked to be homemade butter. In the top drawer I found a butter knife. Slathering fatty gold onto the almost perfect bread slice, I took a bite. Out of sheer willpower, I forced myself not to scarf down the rest of the loaf, it was bread just to die for. It was so good, you could eat it like ice cream, and never have enough. It almost makes me want to kidnap this woman, I thought,, and force her to be my personal chef. Unlike her, though, I have standards.

The time was around five in the afternoon, but it felt more like three in the morning. I was finding it almost impossible to stay focused.

Trudging my way back to the dungeon, I saw the monster was still unconscious on the floor. She looked peaceful, lying there next to her dead sex toy. Honestly her makeup was well done too. She looked like a fallen angel. The teeth on this woman were amazing – no chips, or puffed gums, and just pearly white. Her hair was in a bun, apparently so it wouldn't get in the way when torturing her victims. Even her nails were shaped like small spears. If she weren't insane, we could likely be good friends.

Just to make sure she doesn't kill me in my sleep, I tapped her face with my shoe a few times to make sure she really was out. The metal table behind me looked really comfortable, much better than sleeping on the floor like these other scum.

11: Wish Granted

I AWOKE STANDING IN FRONT OF THE WOMAN. She was hanging hogtied over the table. Every inch of her back was covered in lashes. Her arms had cuts that ran from shoulder to elbow, some being deep enough to see the other side. Shards of glass were forced into her thighs and calves. Bruising and strangle marks covered her neck, but were overshadowed but the cut throat. Taking a closer look, I saw something stuffed in between her cheeks. Still wearing the gloves, I pulled out something squishy and yellow. It was a peep. Lifting her head up, a peep could be seen stuffed down her windpipe. The mascara was ruined by the tears that rolled down her face, leaving it to mix in with the pool of blood on the floor. The red was spread to every corner of the room.

"So what do you think?" It sounded pleased.

"It's... It's... It's horrific. Nauseating. I-I-I," wishing this wasn't real.

"I know, isn't it great!"

"No... no, it's monstrous." Still hoping this was a dream.

"I- what- But I just did what you were thinking?"

"No! No! I was going to hand her over to the police, not kill her. Never, she was-"

"A killer, you saw the souvenirs in the closest. For God sakes, she literally killed someone right before you got here!"

"That's not the point!" I screamed. "I- we- can't do this. There are rules."
172

"Rules? This perverted maniac killed over twenty people. What did the rules do for them?"

"Don't do that!"

"This world has nothing but rules that do nothing except hurt the innocent. Every day I have to listen to the weak. Hear them talk about what's new in fashion, or how their boyfriend cheated on them. It's agony. I just want to cut their throats to end their worthless lives. You believe in Heaven? Well we're Hell!"

I didn't know what to say.

"Without me, you would still be looking over your poor little mommy, making sure that daddy doesn't hurt her."

"Stop it. Shut up! Shut up! Shut! Up!"

"Every fucking night Bang! Bang! Bang! And it only got harder and harder, until I stepped in and made you and that psycho bitch's life better. You think it's a fucking tragedy your daddy died. Get over yourself, he was a piece of shit that would do anything for booze, and every night he would come home looking to blame someone else for his failures. You think I'm psychotic, open your eyes and see the devastation society has formed around you!"

"Shut up!" I tried opening the door, but it was jammed.

"You can't even console your own mother. When was the last time you gave her a hug, visited her, even talked to her?"

"I can't! And because of you! That look in her eyes. What you did ... I- I- I ... You made her and everyone think I was crazy. They strapped me up and locked me in a fucking white room!"

Taking a few steps back to open the door, I found it was solidly locked. I rammed it as hard as I could, again, then again.

"You need to accept the fact that life is always going to screw you over."

The door opened. Out I dashed. Racing down the staircase, my ears screamed with hatred. Running down the street, it looked like a snowstorm was coming. The same bum from the street corner was there again, begging for spare change.

"The weak stand tall, trying to be one of us."

"Spare change?" the bum was now following me.

"No, please just go away." I was trying to hold my temper.

"Spare change, sir?" holding out his hat.

"Did I say I have spare change? Do I look like I give a shit about giving my money to the likes of you?" I shoved his hat back into his face.

I was pushing past the crowded sidewalk, and people purposely tried to bump into me, just to piss me off.

"Watch it!" one man in a purple blazer said.

"Why don't you shut the fuck up!?" I wanted to reach for the gun.

This city and its people are revolting. The snow, black muck in the streets. The piss and shit smell in the air. Women standing outside to make ends meet. Men rummaging in the trash to fill their empty stomachs. Children forced to pick pockets to survive. Watching these people living their worthless lives, not seeing the damned future, it's pathetic. This whole world is pathetic.

Walking into the front entrance of my work, the room smelled of narcissistic betrayal. Everyone had on their fake smiles. Talking and laughing as if they really cared. Given the chance, every last one of them would stab each other in the back. Two men sat next to the coffee stand smiling, making small talk. What would it be like if they didn't just talk about bullshit, and just said the truth?

"Would you like extra sugar with a side of I don't give a shit?"

"Yeah, and just so you know, I've been screwing your wife for the last three months."

"That's great, I hope you didn't wear a condom, because I gave her chlamydia."

"Wonderful."

"Yep, I got it on my honeymoon from this sad-looking hooker."

"Well, everything's going to work out. You'll see."

"Go fuck yourself, John."

"You as well."

They both laughed hysterically.

The elevator doors slid open, and a clutch of people walked out. Pressing the number 58, I watched as the doors started to close. With only an inch left, someone sticks their hand in the elevator, causing it to open back up.

Phil walks happily in.

"Bro, you trying a new look?"

"Hey." I was instantly pissed off that I had to see him.

"Ey, dude, we need to go out and get some drinks. It will be awesome. Okay, so a few nights ago, dude,

I went to this sweet underground speakeasy place. It was like totally wicked. Like we-"

"Phil, can you please just be quiet for a second. I'm kind of having a bad day, and I just... need a bit of silence." I tried to bury the anger.

"Cool, cool, cool. Okay, but first let me tell you about this chick I hooked up with last night. Okay, so she was looking at me from across the room-"

"Dammit, Phil! If you don't shut the fuck up, I'll shove each and every one of your pencils so far up your ass, you'll be tasting eraser for a month!" feeling the vein on my forehead pop up.

"Wow dude, I'm just trying to brighten your day. Chill out," he said, getting defensive.

"Wouldn't it be nice to just break that oversized mouth?"

"SHUT UP!"

Phil inched to the back corner of the elevator.

There was a long silence. At one point Phil took a deep breath.

"Do you want me to break your jaw?" I was getting white-knuckled.

The doors opened up for Phil's floor. He stood there looking at me.

"Get out." I was not leaving any option for interpretation in my voice.

"Yep, yeah, sorry!" he rushed out. Another person tried to walk in. "Don't!" Phil warned him.

The elevator doors close. No music played in the background. Reaching for my own music, I noticed finally that it was gone.

"Looking for something?" It asked.

"You really must hate me."

"On the contrary, I'm saving you from yourself."

There was no point in arguing.

"Did you know, in Africa, some tribes will spit on one another as a way of saying hello?"

Silence.

"Of course you did." It persisted. I steeled myself.

Silence.

"Why is that whenever I'm making myself known, it's okay for you to be a dominating asshole, but whenever I do, then something 'bad' happens?"

"Maybe it's because I'm the bad guy," I thought. "No, that's just entrepreneurship shining through your depressing darkness. You and I, we are like bourbon and scotch. Both fine whiskeys, except one of them has a much better aroma to it."

The elevator door opened. One of the secretaries walked by and saw me. She looked at me as if I were a ghost. Walking to my office, I saw people staring at me as I passed them.

"Jinny, can you get me the reports on the Luxen account?" I said to my own secretary.

And I slammed my door behind me.

Pacing back and forth, I threw everything off my desk. Jinny walked in quietly, making herself look small.

"What?" I wanted to shoot the next person who didn't give me a straight answer.

She was mortified.

She ran out before she could say anything. They know what it did. Somehow they know!

The look in everyone's eyes... That look of unbending fear. They no longer saw me for me. Instead, they saw the monster. It's an insult. I'm not him, I will never be him! He is unhinged, unbalanced, certifiably insane. As far as I'm concerned, these people can burn. Let them rot in hell. Let the demons rip them limb from limb, make them stand in molten rock and slowly cook for the devil's next meal. How dare they suggest such a simple-minded thought!

"Kill them. All of them. Just – Let – Go." Its voice itched my brain. "Do it. They all hate you. Listen to them. They don't understand. Do it!"

"No!"

The gun was in my hand, pointing at the door, trigger finger itching. Jinny peeked her head in. Quickly hiding the gun behind my back, I watched her walk in, tears rolling down her face.

"Okay, it's not what you think," I said.

She walked up close to me and gave me a hug. My body tensed up.

"I'm so sorry." Her tears soaked into my suit lapels.

"It's okay, you can get off me now." I pushing her away, confused about why she was apologizing.

"No, the police just called." And she became hysterical.

"Hey, Jinny! Jinny!" snapping my fingers to get her attention. "What did the police say?" Afraid that someone blabbed about the misunderstanding.

"It's obvious, you just heard!" she couldn't stop crying.

"Okay, I need you to take a deep breath and tell me what the police said."

"Your mother is dead," she choked.

Did she really say that? My mother is dead? My mother is dead? My Mother Is Dead. No. It just didn't sound right. My mother is dead. My mother is dead. No, my mother is not dead. My mother is dead. It slid off the tongue with ease, but the word dead, well, it had a crack to it. The sound made my heart pound. Or did I not hear her correctly? "Your mother hit her head?" maybe. Well, in that case, depending on how severe the injury was, I could still pull the plug. No, she had definitely said "Your mother is dead."

"Get out." I whispered.

"I-"

"Get out."

The door made a loud creak as it shut behind her. The room outside was silent. No mumbles outside, not even a sniffle. Getting a glass and bottle from my desk drawer, I poured myself a drink.

"Lib?" It sounded worried.

Preferably, there would be ice in the glass, but if I went to fetch some, everyone would be staring, asking me if I was okay. Sitting on top of my desk, I sipped my drink neat. The sound of silence has been a distant friend – until now.

"Stop being a voiceless pig and answer me!" It shouted.

This life has been nothing but absolute shit. Being tossed aside. Forced to live amongst the insane. Going as far as destroying my body and mind to find a solution to this crippling woe. But now the puppeteer is dead, and no one is left to pull the strings. Let there be light in eternal darkness.

"Listen to me, this doesn't change anything. Look outside. See all the weak. See how they are blind to the truth. That life is a game of wits ... and you and I stand tall. To us, they are nothing more than ants, ready to be squashed, for our amusement. Look and see what you have accomplished here. If we work together, this whole skyscraper will be a toy to us."

I walked out. Leaving the office, everyone was staring.

Backtracking over to Jinny's desk, I asked her, "Do you know where the boss is?" calmly whispering.

"Um," she said shuffling through her papers, "she is in the conference room, with the board of directors."

"Thank you," I said, with a smile on my face.

The blinds were shut on the doors and windows. I knocked on the door, and there was no response. Where do people get off not having the decency of letting someone in. If they think it's okay to ignore me, they are sorely mistaken. Forcing myself into the conference room, I saw why the lights were dimmed, as my boss and her receptionist were casually breaking in the table.

They were caught off guard, and jumped behind some chairs.

"Hey, just a heads up, I quit. I'd say it was a pleasure, but it seems you already have that under control," I said, feeling perfectly comfortable with what I'd just walked in on.

"What! Stop! Go back!" I really didn't need this from It, not now. "Tell her it was a joke. Blackmail her to get her job." Nope. I was done.

The elevator seemed to move a lot quicker than usual. Walking outside, I saw the snowfall was becoming more intense by the minute. It was compact and the sidewalk was basically ice. The bum was sitting in his cardboard box, trying to find a bit of warmth. When he saw me, he turned himself into a ball. Opening up my wallet, I noted there was a wad of cash and credit cards, along with my ID. I removed my ID and I handed the bum the wallet.

"Here." I showed him all the cash.

He slowly reached for it. Once he had a grip, he snatched it from my hands, and shoved it down his pants. The apartment keys were in my coat pocket. I handed them over. He took those as well.

"Have fun." I left him with enough money to score a few lines of coke.

The cold wind numbed my cheeks as I made my way back to the apartment. Running my fingers through my hair, I felt pieces of ice starting to develop.

There was a spare key in the wall light next to my door. I opened my closet; there were too many options. Sweaters. Blazers. Button-ups. Overcoats. Boots. Brogue shoes and wingtip shoes. Khakis. Dockers. But not one pair of jeans. Pushing it all aside, I found there was a plastic bag. Ripping it open I found inside was a worn-out navy blue hoodie, gray sweatpants, and a pair of sneakers. Removing all my clothing except socks and underwear, I slipped into the new attire. It felt-- loose.

Grabbing my ID and car keys, I opened the front door. Two police officers were blocking my exit.

This was very frustrating. Taking a deep breath, I greeted the policemen. "Hello officers, how may I help you?" I was wearing my vexing smile.

"Are you Mr. Sherwood?" one of them asked.

"Nope, just house sitting, I'm afraid." I tried to push past them.

"Can we see some form of identification?" the other officer asked.

"Of course," patting my front pockets, then the back. "Must have lost it."

"Sir, we're gonna need you to come with us."

"Why- I didn't do anything wrong?" I couldn't get defensive.

"Sir," trying to put his hand on my shoulder.

"Don't touch me!" I slapped it away.

The other cop took his gun out and pointed it at my chest. "Get on the ground! Now! Get on the ground!"

The other one grabbed the handcuffs off his belt. Taking a step back, he moved back into the doorway, blocking his partner's aim, and without hesitation, I punched him in the throat, causing him to fall to his knees, just before I rammed hard into him, which forced him to fall on top of his partner.

The officer on the floor got on his radio. "Ten-thirty-three, officer down, suspect on foot!"

Racing down the street, I knew I needed to blend in with the crowd. Changing speeds, I pushed myself into the center of mass of people on the sidewalk and slowed it. The parking garage was just a few blocks away. It was getting dark. Traffic was starting to speed up.

"You're ruining everything. Go back to the police station so we can sort this out."

I threw the hood up over my head. As IF I needed Its advice now.

"Listen to me! No damage has been done; this is still salvageable," It said optimistically.

"I just assaulted a police officer. How is that in any way salvageable?"

There was a moment of silence.

"You really know how to fuck things up, don't you? Kudos for releasing some of that built-up anger. But tell me, if you didn't go there to kill that woman, what did you think you were going to do?"

"I told you, take her to the police and hand her over."

The people around me were starting to stare.

"Fascinating, you still lie to me even after this complete and utterly ridiculous blunder."

"No matter what I say," I argued back at him, "you will still be the aggressor. By now I thought you'd be pathetically crying in the darkest part of my subconscious."

"Life does like to play the role of cruel bitch," It chuckled. "But there is nothing to do now except wait for the damned to be sent to hell and be doled out their punishments."

The car was on the fifth floor of the parking garage. I started the engine and sped down the garage ramps, cutting off several taxis. The gun was still in my waistband, poking me in my back. Setting it over in the passenger seat, I punched on the radio. Every station was static. Going up. Going down the stations, just the sound of feedback. I smacked the radio. Realistically, I thought, that wasn't going to work, but then the beautiful harmonies of classical music flowed into my ears. Out the exit, hard right, down the street, edge of town ... It was impossible to see the stars in the night sky with the goliath-sized snowstorm overhead.

Several hours passed, I was still doing a steady 90 mph or better, but fuel was running low. All of these drivers on the road were either one foot in the grave assholes or tin-toed fools. Passing a speed limit sign, it said 65 mph and the speedometer in the dash lights said 97. A cop with eagle eyes must have spotted me, because now I saw tiny blue and red lights flashing in the distance behind me.

By this time, I was driving alongside a forest. The fuel tank was basically empty, the needle on the gauge below the E point. Pulling over to the side of the road, I could see a swarm of blue and red lights closing in on me. The wind whined around the windows and rocked the whole car. It was nearly impossible to see anything with the horizontal snow and ice blowing over the hood and the back window, but as I climbed out, crunching on the snow, the moonlight was able to shine just bright enough to lead me into the icy depths of the forest at the edge of the highway.

12: Farewell My Friend

AS I STEPPED INTO THE EDGE OF THE FOREST, the storm came to a whispered halt. Each step was an inch deeper. It didn't take long and I was knee-deep in snow. My socks were damp, my toes numb. Not long after, frostbite started to kick in.

All the trees looked the same, pain hiding behind rage. Their long arms reached out, waiting to pull a soul into their own terror-filled wonderland, leaving them preserved for summer. Food for worms.

One of the most fascinating things about darkness is the fear. A monster under the bed. The boogeyman staring through the closet shades. A cold sharp pain running down your neck. Standing out in this forest, though, that feeling was absent, and all that was left was the next few minutes.

The sounds of barking dogs and sirens were gradually closing in. My feet couldn't move any farther. Finally falling to the ground, I leaned up against the frozen bark of a log next to me. Breathing became the primary focus, and I finally swallowed the barrel of the gun.

The dark slithering pain is never as fun as it seems. To put the feeling in words will never give them justice. A person standing outside of understanding will attempt to hear and feel for them, but to comprehend dejection is impossible. The irony of it all is that the members feel outcasted, forced out, even though for most, it's all in their heads. For most. When they finally succumb to society's peer pressure and the crush of the ridiculous, they pump themselves with chemicals, seeing a person they no longer recognize, no longer a man or woman, just a puppet with fraying strings. The occasional rare patient will feel bright changes, but for others, for most, the darkness is all that is left.

"Please... don't."

Pulling the trigger. There was an echoing crack as the bullet ran up through my skull; it tore apart all the dreadful memories, destroyed all the suffering caused by my hand and others' and leaving behind just a hole inside a downed log, filled with bits and pieces of bone and hair and brain.

Epilogue

LOUD OBNOXIOUS HORNS AND DINGS deafened the sound of college funds being flushed away. Beers were being spilt, making the floor sticky. Machines everywhere shouted out "WINNER." Peering across the labyrinth of the room, you could see several looks in everyone's eyes. The look of pain and wishful desire, knowing if they'd just played a little longer, they could have won their money back. There was the look of the drunken barfly gal, the tired old guy who hadn't laughed while sober for ten years, and the young hopeful guy who hadn't yet earned enough cynicism or pessimism. They play the games not knowing what's going on in front of them, and by morning their pride will be nonexistent, and they'll have nothing except the lint in their pockets. Finally, there are the fuckoffs, and they can be quite enjoyable; they mind their own business, not speaking much or caring about what's going on around them. You can never know what's going on in their heads, because they don't need to express their appreciation for winning or their frustration at loss.

Sitting at a blackjack table sat none of these, instead just darkness bending the limbs of a corpse. To its left was a fuckoff, and to the right were three wishful thinkers, who all felt the need to voice their opinions on every hand dealt out to them.

Cards were dealt. The darkness held an ace and a king, twenty-one. The fuckoff was nice enough to fist-pump the air whenever he or the darkness got

188

twenty-one, and the darkness did the same back as a courtesy. Sadly, though, the fuckoff's cards were just not as lucky this time – he had now a nine and four. Hit me. King. Bust.

The darkness gave him a little nod, as if saying "it's okay."

The next hand was dealt. The people to the right knocked on the table, trying to act like professionals, but it just made them look like thoughtless pigs stomping their ugly hooves.

The cards read a six and a three.

The man at the far right end of the table shouted, "Hey dude, double down!"

Ignoring this, it took a hit instead. Seven, so sixteen now.

"Ey! Stand, trust me, stand!" the man shouted again.

"Hit me," the darkness softly growled.

Jack. Bust.

"You should've listened. Common man, just play the game! I told you!"

This impulsive maggot trying to control what it could and could not do. Annoying.

The fuckoff got twenty-one.

The darkness softly fist-pumped in his direction.

Next hand, two sixes. The darkness decided to split them. Six and a jack. Stand. Next, six, three, and three.

"DOUBLE DOWN!"

The darkness felt its right hand starting to shake, clenching to keep the trimmer under control. It tapped the table two times.

"Why aren't you listening to me!"

The darkness stayed silent, but swiveled eyes slowly toward the brazen fuckoff.

"Hey fuckhead, answer me!"

It continued on with the game.

Two. "Hit me." Five. "Hit me." Two.

"Hey!" the man shouted. "Hey, stand now! Do it! Trust me! Do it!"

"Hit me."

Queen.

"Are you fucking kidding me! Hey dumbass!" It turned slowly to look again at the guy. "Why did you hit? Why not stand like I said?!"

"Because I wanted to. Why does it matter?"

"Why? Because your dumbass is making us all lose. You see these other two guys. We are trying to work together here! So, when one of us wins, we all win! So why don't you sit down, shut the fuck up, and listen to me!"

The darkness could feel its heart pounding out of its chest, shoving both of its hands down in its pockets to control the shaking.

Next hand.

Ten and five.

"Okay, what you need to do here is stand."

The darkness glared at him, then at the cards, then back at the fuckoff guy. "I want to double down." Four. Nineteen now.

"Are you serious right now! Are you trying to piss me off!" his face was turning red.

"I'm just here to play. So if you don't mind ..."

"No! You need to get out of here. No one is having fun anymore, and you're making us all lose. So why don't you leave before you make things worse!"

The darkness just stared at him for the longest time, motionless and silent.

"Leave! Get the fuck out of here!"

It had enough. Collecting the chips, the darkness walked away and headed for a different table.

A few hours later the darkness is standing behind a slot machine, eyeing the small bug that had been so disrespectful. It sees him getting up and walking toward the men's restroom. An overjoyed but painful little smile rolled across its face, slowly following behind.

Postscript

THE ROOM WAS COLD, SPARSELY furnished and dimly lit. A woman in her mid-forties sat in a metal chair, covering her face with bandaged hands, her elbows on the metal table.

She mumbled something over the tears. "It's my fault. It's my fault, it's my fault."

The door in the corner made a loud squeak as the cop walked into the room, carrying two paper cups of stale coffee. Taking his seat across from her, he set her coffee before her.

"Mrs. Sherwood," he said gently. "I have to ask you a few questions, okay, and I want you to take your time. Now walk me through what happened."

She choked out a few words, but it was impossible to make anything from it.

"All right, all right. Mrs. Sherwood, now look at me, okay? Just look at me."

She wiped away tears, and the police officer could see the bruises covering her face and a deep cut across her lower lip. Her eyes were red and puffy.

"Just breathe. Do it with me. A deep breath in ... and out. Deep breath in ... and out. Take your time."

The crying subsided. She rubbed her face.

"All right, now can I get you anything. Water? A sandwich? A coat? I know it's chilly in here ..."

She shook her head.

"All right."

"Okay, now start from the beginning."

She reached for the coffee, her hands shaking, and took a loud sip. "I was making dinner. We were having spaghetti. My son was in the other room

192

reading. His father was in the kitchen with me, making himself another drink. I remember I was stirring the pot of sauce on the stove and I heard a glass break. He had dropped the drink and then knocked the bottle on the floor too. I grabbed a towel and went to pick up the broken glass, and he just got another bottle from the cupboard and was pouring himself another drink. I had a major stupid moment and asked him if he thought that was a good idea. It was stupid of me. He got this mean look on his face, and he set his drink back on the counter and came after me."

She started breathing faster, her eyes wide, sitting up straighter, beginning to hyperventilate.

"Hey- Hey- Hey now," cautioned the cop. "It's okay, it's okay! Just be steady, take your time." He reached both hands across the table toward her. Her eyes locked onto his and she sniffled several times.

Wiping away the tears again, she went on. "I was picking up the glass and one of the pieces cut me. I- I- blood was dripping on the floor. I wiped it up with the towel but more blood was dripping. He yelled at me, saying I'd ruin the hardwood floor. My son, Lib, he called to me to see if everything was okay, and my husband told him to mind his own business. Whenever my husband gets like this, Lib tries to stay out of it. He talks to himself a lot, talks to his imaginary friend."

The cop interrupted. "Whoa wait, his imaginary friend? Your son, how often does he talk to this imaginary friend?"

"I don't know. When he was growing up it seemed like he could have talked to it for hours. I thought it was just a phase, you know, everyone has imaginary friends growing up. And as he got older, he didn't do it as much."

"But he's talked to this imaginary friend since childhood?"

"Yes, I guess so."

"Does his friend have a name?"

"I don't think so. He just is always talking to him, like soft and quietly, but then sometimes loud and he'll yell at him like they're arguing."

"What do they argue about?"

"Oh, I don't really know," she said, frowning, "he just sounds mad sometimes."

"Okay, carry on."

She wiped her eyes again. "Sorry, where was I?"

"You cut yourself and you were bleeding."

"Oh right, yes, and then I smelled smoke. The garlic bread in the oven was burning. I was stupid, I shouldn't have forgotten about the bread, and I went to pull it out of the oven and burned my hands. I was upset, I guess, and trying to make everything okay again. What I remember at that point is my husband yelling that I was a 'fucking idiot' and saying how all I ever do is make a mess. I was trying to clean up the blood and I kept saying sorry over and over, and running my hands under cold water in the sink. I heard my son get up and come in to help me, but he got yelled at to go sit down.

I took the bread out of the oven. It was really black. He took one look at it and saw what I'd done, and I took a step back to get some space and I guess my hand went over the pan on the stove and a couple drops of blood fell into the sauce. That did it. He started yelling. He threw his glass at me, hard, and it hit me in the face. I grabbed the closest thing I could reach to protect myself – a big lid. But he grabbed it from me and threw it at the wall. My son was back now, and asked if he could help somehow. I was about to say everything was all right, when my husband yelled at him to shut up. I tried to calm him down but he threw me against the wall. I hit my head pretty hard and fell to the floor. I tried crawling away, but he dragged me back. I screamed. Lib walked in and saw the mess everywhere, and I begged him to just leave ..." She started crying again, wailing now with the memory.

"It's okay," the cop whispered, "just breathe."

She tried taking a few breaths in, tears dripping down onto the table.

"Take your time. It's okay. Now what happened next?"

"My son, he uh- he tried to help me. Tried to calm his father down. But he punched Lib, and he fell to the floor. I could see him mouth something from the ground, but his dad kicked him. He- he kicked Lib over and over. I begged him to stop. I screamed. I grabbed some of the broken glass from the sink and threw it at his head. He turned around, and the look in his eyes, I knew what was coming. He grabbed my shirt and raised his fist ... I closed my eyes, terrified. But nothing happened. I heard a grunt, and my eyes opened and I saw that Lib had grabbed onto his arm.

So he dropped me and swung at Lib. I tried grabbing onto him to stop him, and he ran his fingers across his mouth and looked at the blood. Then everything just happened so quickly. I told Lib to run, but he said 'Lib isn't here right now' and smiled at me. I- I- I didn't know what he meant. Lib- he grabbed the bottle sitting on the table and broke it, crashed it on the edge of the table. There was so much blood! And he was laughing! Blood, it was on the floor, on me, on the table, it was everywhere! I tried to cover my ears and Lib dragged my husband into our bedroom, and I couldn't figure out what I was hearing. But when Lib came back out his hands, his hands and arms were covered in blood."

The cop reached over again and patted her hand. "And then what?" he asked. She looked at him, her eyes red-rimmed and wide, and she said, "I don't know. I don't know what happened. Honestly, after I saw Lib was covered in blood I just guess I checked out for a while, I don't know what happened. I remember lights outside and cops yelling and knocking on the door and that's all I remember till I got here. But please, it's not his fault! He couldn't survive in prison. Please!"

"Ma'am I don't decide who's to blame."

"Please! You have to help me! Blame me, not him!"

Months later, Lib is standing in a courtroom, being eyed by a judge.

"Your honor, clearly the events that took place were driven by the intent of self-defense. Looking at the photos of the mother's face, the split on her lip and the bruising around her eyes – this was quite plainly no accident. My client made the decision to intervene, to de-escalate the situation, to protect his mother from an attack. When the attacker struck my client, he fought back to protect himself, to protect his mother. This young man right here was viciously assaulted; he sustained numerous injuries, broken ribs, a concussion; the attacker broke his nose."

The prosecutor jumped from his seat. "Your honor, while we do sympathize with the defendant, that doesn't excuse the fact that he killed another man."

"To defend his mother and himself!"

"The evidence shows his actions were animalistic, far beyond self-defense. This was intentional murder, no matter the motivation."

"Which is why we are pleading not guilty on the basis of insanity. He states several times over in the police interrogations that he was not in control at the time of the attack, not aware, and he said someone else was commanding his body. His mother stated that he has been talking to the voice in his head since childhood. This man doesn't deserve to be punished for his illness – he needs to be helped."

The judge brooded for a long pause, looked at the lawyers, looked again at the photos, the defendant, and finally back at the lawyers. "Based on the evidence presented here, this man is dangerous. He took matters into his own hands and enacted his own form of justice. The evidence itself tells an appalling story. Never have I seen something as mortifying and gruesome as this case and its violent aftermath. But if all we do is punish men and women for sins that could have been prevented through communicative action, then I no longer wish to be a part of the judicial system. Sadly, not enough of us step forward and speak the bitter truth, and seeing what I've seen today, hearing what I've heard, I have only one choice. Liberation Sherwood, I sentence you to be institutionalized, confined at the state hospital until such time as you are deemed sane, if or when that day comes, till you are reasonably assessed to no longer be a danger to society."

www.ingramcontent.com/pod-product-compliance
Lightning Source LLC
Chambersburg PA
CBHW060149130626
46556CB00006B/2563